BIGFOOT CRANK STOMP

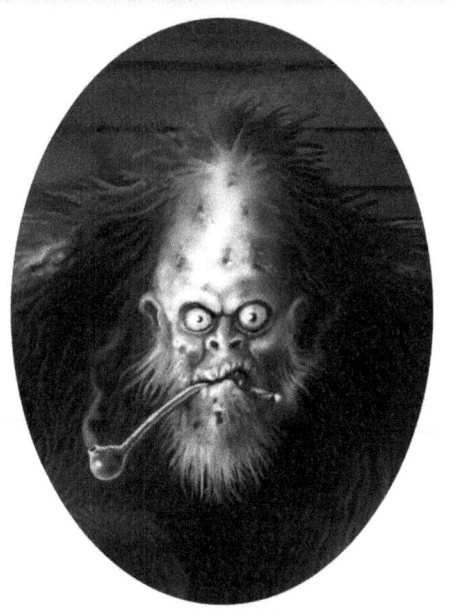

ERIK WILLIAMS

deadite press

DEADITE PRESS
205 NE BRYANT
PORTLAND, OR 97211
www.DEADITEPRESS.com

AN ERASERHEAD PRESS COMPANY
www.ERASERHEADPRESS.com

ISBN: 978-1-62105-085-8

Copyright © 20123 by Erik Williams

Cover art copyright © 2013 Hauke Vagt

All rights reserved. No part of this book may be reproduced or transmitted in any form or by any means, electronic or mechanical, including photocopying, recording, or by any information storage and retrieval system, without the written consent of the publisher, except where permitted by law.

Printed in the USA.

Acknowledgments

Special thanks to Kim Despins, Kurt Dinan, and the entire Snutch Labs crew; Shane McKenzie; Edward Lee; Thunderstorm Books; and John Skipp.

Super special thanks to the team at Deadite Press for making this writer guy feel welcome and putting out one bad ass book with one bad ass cover.

Finally, super super special thanks to Sam W. Anderson for being my Pinko Commie and Norman Partridge for saving my career.

For Dad.
Thanks for introducing me to the wonders of B-movies.
Not sure if that was a good thing in the long run,
but thanks all the same!

PROLOGUE

"Holy shit it fucking killed Jimmy!"

"I know it killed Jimmy! Now help me get these chains back on!"

"It just pushed him down and stomped on his head. Fucking stomped his head into mush man!"

Waylon reared back and slung his arm and slapped Stan as hard as he could. Sounded like lightning splitting a hundred-year-old oak. Stan's face snapped to the right and his long hair whipped all the way back around his head. His glasses flew off.

There was silence for a moment. Then from inside the cabin the TV's audio destroyed the peace, blaring a commercial for a show called *River Monsters*.

"I said I know. Now help me get these fucking chains back on!"

Stan blinked and crawled and felt around in the dirt and gravel for his glasses. Waylon turned to Bud and Cam. They stood several feet away, empty Tupperware bowls in their hands. Shaking. In the cabin, the intro for *Meerkat Manor* started.

"Help me!"

Bud blinked and dropped the bowl and hurried forward. Cam just stood there.

Waylon grabbed the first set of heavy chains and pulled them together and snapped the lock in place. Bud handed him the next. The narrator of *Meerkat Manor* spoke low enough that Waylon could actually hear something other than the program. Below the door—below him—he could hear it snorting. Snorting. Snorting. Panicked. Like it couldn't get enough. Like if it couldn't get one more nostrilful it was going to die.

He snapped the next lock closed. Then the third and the fourth in rapid succession. Once the fifth was in place, he backed away with Bud until they were next to Cam. Stan found his glasses and jumped to his feet and sprinted over to them.

"It's snoring, man," Stan said. "I heard it snoring. I think we're okay."

"For now." Waylon half expected the cellar door to explode into a million splinters and the chains to snap one link after the next.

"How could you hear it snoring over the TV?" Bud said.

"I swear I did."

"This isn't fun anymore," Cam said, bowl still shaking in his hand.

"What happened down there?" Bud said. "We gave it our dose no problem. Seemed satisfied."

"Guess Jimmy's wasn't enough."

"That hasn't been a problem so far."

"Well it is now, ain't it?" Waylon rubbed his eyes. "We were late on the feeding and its tolerance is growing. It needs more."

"Christ we already give it three bowls of crank a day."

"Then we give it four. Spread it throughout the day instead of all at once."

"That's a lot of product we're wasting and we have a deadline to meet."

"You don't think I fucking know that?"

Bud held up his hands for calm. "I'm just saying we've got the Cacheros expecting their load in two days and we're only three-quarters of the way to filling it. We start diverting more to that fucking thing and we're going to be lucky to meet our quota. And you know what the Cacheros will do to us. Jimmy will be the lucky one."

"What do you suggest?"

"Kill it."

Waylon chewed his bottom lip. "How?"

"Shoot it. Next dose, we hand it over and when it leans in we pop cap in its fucking head."

"I'm not going anywhere close to that thing," Cam said. "I say we leave it down there and burn the place down around it."

"We have to finish the load," Waylon said. "We can't pack shop and leave until then."

"Then we shoot it," Bud said.

"I'm not going anywhere close—"

"I heard you the fucking first time!"

"You're both right," Waylon said.

"What?" Bud and Cam said simultaneously.

"I don't want to risk opening that door again. We might be able to feed it but it also might snap on us as soon as we open it. The thing's gone full fiend. Plus we can't risk it escaping and going bugfuck nuts on any locals. We need to handle it but we need to get the load done first. How long before we finish if we don't divert anymore to it, Stan?"

"Got to feed the need," Stan said.

Waylon snapped his fingers. "Hey how long?"

Stan blinked and shifted from the cellar door. "Twelve hours with what we've got cooking right now. Should have enough to feed it one more bowl if necessary."

"Okay." Waylon rubbed the back of his neck. "We grind until we're done. Let the fucker starve down there. As soon as we have the load finished we pack-up the Jeep and light the fucking cabin on fire and head for the meet."

"What about the equipment?" Bud said.

"Leave it."

"But—"

"It's old junk we swiped anyway. With this deal we'll make enough to buy good equipment."

"And the lab?"

"Need to move anyway. Mickey Dolan's sniffing around. Won't be long until he makes a move against us. So we zig before he can zag."

Bud nodded. Cam merely shrugged. Stan stared at the cellar door.

"All right, let's grind," Waylon said. "Stan, go ahead and start prepping another bowl just in case we need it. Cam, the TV needs to be louder."

"It's as loud as it'll go."

"Fine. But put it on something other than *Animal Planet*. I'm sick of fucking *Animal Planet*." Waylon motioned at the cabin. "If you got to take a piss or something do it now. Everyone in the lab in five minutes."

RUSSELL

"Are you ready to fucking do this?"

Russell cracked a knuckle and shook his head. "I don't know, man."

"What the fuck you mean you don't know?"

Russell rubbed his mouth and turned to Mickey, staring at him in the darkness of the Ford F-150's cab, the whites visible in the moonlight. His sunken eyes didn't blink. They burrowed into Russell's and when he couldn't meet them any longer he looked at the dashboard instead.

"You're sure this has to happen this way?"

Mickey pointed through the windshield with his chin at the log cabin at the top of the long driveway, his boney hands squeezing the peeling leather of the steering wheel tight. "They cooking glass in there, Russell. We got to send a message to these motherfuckers this is our turf. We don't, we gonna have skinheads and beaners and fucking god knows what up here in our neck of the woods cooking. And then we get squeezed out."

"We're small time, Mickey. There's enough turf to go around."

"Yeah, we small time. And unless we take control of this situation, we gonna be no time. Feel me?"

"I don't know man."

"You need to change that attitude right quick. I'm going up there. If you ain't with me, then you against me. And if you against me..." Mickey lifted his .45 from the seat and brushed a stray hair from his forehead with the barrel. "This relationship is gonna change. And not for the better. At least not for you."

"Fuck, man, you don't have to threaten me." Russell swallowed a mouthful of spit. "I'm with you, Mickey, so chill."

"I'm chill. You ain't gotta worry about that."

"I'm just wondering how you know there's people in there cooking."

"You questioning my intel?"

"No. But I want to be sure. You know, keep the heat off us as much as possible. We kill cookers, nobody's going to care much. We kill some family or some San Fran faggots on vacation, the heat is going to be hot and fierce."

Mickey laughed. "Check out Russell being all logical and shit."

"It ain't funny."

"No, it ain't. And neither are you."

"What?"

"You're a terrible liar. Always have been. That shit ain't funny."

Russell rubbed his stomach. "Hell what do you expect? You drag me up here and tell me we got to kill a bunch of people. Then you say if I don't I can pretty much kiss my ass goodbye. So yeah, I'm trying to figure a way out of this shit without anyone dying."

Mickey put a Marlboro in the right corner of his mouth and lit it with the flame from his Zippo. "That's real good, Russell."

"What's that?"

"Your honesty. Normally I'd hear your bullshit for about an hour before getting the truth. This is progress."

"Shit." Russell looked out the window. "Doesn't matter much either way, does it?"

Mickey exhaled, filling the cab with smoke. "No."

"Who are they?"

"Couple of high school drop outs thought it would be easier to get rich cooking meth than staying in school. Saw it on some TV show. It's got to be easy if it's on TV right? So they broke bad."

"And we can't scare them off?"

"Not these boys. We could beat them dreadful and they'd come back for more. Young and dumb, know what I mean?"

"Yeah. We used to be them."

"True. But we got in the game when there was no competition up here. Now there is. Territory is vital to our survival. People staking claims all over NorCal. We don't hold our ground, we done and dead. So you see we got to nip this in the butt now."

Russell pulled his pipe from his jacket and loaded up a couple of rocks and sparked up. He closed his eyes and inhaled deep and let the meth make magic.

"Not smart," Mickey said. "It fucks up your focus."

"It helps my confidence." Russell exhaled and opened his eyes, already feeling his nerves relax. "You want me to do this then I need to do *this*."

"Just don't shoot me in the fucking back."

Russell offered him the pipe.

"Keep it to yourself. I need to stay sharp."

Russell shrugged and took another hit. "How many people inside?" Smoke rode his words.

"Three. Maybe four, tops. Nothing too complicated."

"That's two more than us. Not good for hand guns."

"I've got shotguns in the bed."

Russell set the pipe on the dashboard. His head felt clearer. His vision sharpened. His muscles twitched. The adrenaline started to course down his hands and legs. Yeah, he was ready. As ready as he'd ever be.

He eyed Mickey's .45. He could run. Maybe he'd be fast enough to get out of the truck before Mickey blew his brains out. Maybe.

But Russell didn't like his chances. Not with Mickey this sure of what had to happen. They'd grown up together but that didn't mean shit when Mickey was set on something. Nope, when he had his mind set he either got his way or went fucking crazy. Make a move the wrong way, and Russell's ass would be in a shallow grave in a few hours. Better to get high and kill some people and go home.

"How we going in?"

Mickey lit up another Marlboro. "Through the front door."

"Both of us?"

"I scouted it last night. The back door's a sheet of plywood nailed to the frame. Probably thought it was better having one working door. Easier to defend if someone broke in."

"Stupid. Only one way out, too."

"Yeah but lucky us. So I go in and you hang back and take out any who jump out a window. Easy enough."

"Sure."

"Maybe I get them all and no one jumps out and you get to keep your hands clean. See, things already looking up."

Mickey laughed. Russell didn't.

"How much do you think they got in there?" Russell said.

"Glass or cash?"

"Either."

"Well considering their product is shit, let's not entertain the glass aspect. Cash wise, based on what I've seen and heard, maybe twenty large."

"That's it?"

"I told you they was just starting up. Gotta get them before they get big. They get big, they can afford protection."

"I get half."

"You dictating the percentage?"

Russell rubbed his neck, his throat dry. "I need to make some payments."

"I thought you settled that."

Russell bit his tongue and tried to clear his head and not think of his mom. "Nah. Still got a few. Radiation treatments ain't cheap."

"Right." Mickey stubbed out his Marlboro in the overflowing ashtray. "Fifty makes you happy, fifty it is."

"Well, let's do this," Russell said. "Before my high wears off."

They got out and eased the doors shut until they heard a faint click. Mickey lifted a tarp in the bed. Underneath was a plastic bin holding two twelve-gauge pumps and a bunch of loose shells. He grabbed both guns and handed one to Russell.

Russell scooped up a handful of .00 buck shells and started loading. Mickey followed suit.

The air was cool and still. Smelled of a camp fire or two. Not tourist season so the smoke wasn't thick. Good thing, too, or this whole operation would turn into a police shootout in no time.

Russell looked at the top of the trees. The Douglas Firs bent slightly. A small wind coming down into the valley but nothing low to the ground. Too bad. A lower wind would rustle branches enough to mask their movements. No such luck tonight.

"Got any water?" Russell said.

"No."

Russell rubbed his throat. "Fucking cottonmouth."

"Should have thought about that before sparking up."

Russell let it go, trying to swallow what little saliva he could. "Only dudes up there right?"

"What?"

"Only dudes right?"

"Yeah as far as I know."

"No women or children."

"Are you fucking deaf? I said only dudes as far as I know."

"What's that mean?"

"That means I'm pretty sure they all guys but maybe one of them called a hooker or kidnapped a kid. It means I don't fucking know everything."

Russell held up his free hand. "All right, man. Don't get all pissy. I just don't want to be killing no women or kids."

"Unless the money's good, right?"

"Fuck you."

"If there's enough to pay your ma's medical bills for a few months, you'd probably stomp an infant to death."

Russell spat and raised the shotgun and pointed it at Mickey's chest. "Shut the fuck up, man."

Mickey grinned. "That piss you off, me talking that way about your ma?"

"Fucking A right it does."

"Get the blood up? Make you want to kill me?"

"Yeah."

"Good. Now let's direct that anger toward more productive pursuits."

"Fuck you." Russell lowered the shotgun and turned

toward the house. "Lead the way, asshole."

"There's the Russell I went into business with."

"And you still the ruthless prick I grew up with."

Mickey chuckled as he started up the long winding driveway. Russell walked to his right. They didn't speak, the only sound their breathing and footfalls on gravel and clay.

As they neared the log cabin, Russell heard laughter and conversation. Then applause. He froze in place and listened. Mickey kept walking. It took Russell another moment to realize it was a TV turned up. Way up. He shook his head, feeling dumb, and caught up to Mickey.

"Sounds like *Seinfeld*," Mickey said. "At least we don't gotta worry about them hearing us coming."

"Yeah."

"Remember that one where Kramer was using butter as tanning oil?" Mickey chuckled. "Fucking stupid ass Kramer."

"The one where he got sun burnt." Russell smiled despite himself. "Smelled like dinner."

"And Newman started drooling and shit."

They both chuckled some more as they neared the cabin.

It seemed like every light was on in the place. All the windows were shut and blinds drawn. No shadows passed. Smoke billowed from the chimney. Smelled like burning pine.

The TV audience applauded and the *Seinfeld* theme kicked in. It faded and an erectile dysfunction commercial blared down the driveway. If it lasts longer than four hours, call a doctor.

"Who the fuck listens to the TV that loud?" Russell said and rubbed his mouth with the back of his free hand.

"Maybe they're in another room and couldn't hear it."

"Can hear it on the other side of the county."

"Who the fuck cares? All that matters is they can't hear us, right?"

"Sure." But Russell didn't like it. It didn't sit right. Nobody listens to a TV that loud.

Mickey crouched down behind the front of a beat-up Jeep Wrangler. Russell followed suit, casting a glance down the driveway from where they'd come. Empty and black.

"Okay, young man," Mickey said. "Let's do this."

Russell shifted in his squat. "What about after?"

"What you mean after?"

"We're going to have to beat feet back down the driveway. Someone calls the cops, that's the way they're coming. Only one way in and out."

"Ain't no one calling no cops. Ain't nobody up here this time of year other than cookers."

"Maybe. Maybe some camper hears the gunshots and makes the call."

"They won't know the house. By the time the cops figure it out, we'll be long gone."

"Still, we should have parked closer. As it is now we got a lot of ground to cover just to get back to the truck."

Mickey looked down the dark driveway. "Shit, you fucking right. Why the fuck didn't you say something before we got all the way the fuck up here?"

Russell shrugged. "Just occurred to me."

"Well your timing sucks." Mickey spat. "Shit. Guess we gonna do this quick then. Not that we weren't before but no lingering. We in, we out. And don't touch nothing unless we taking it."

"This ain't my first rodeo, Mickey."

"Go on over to the side of the cabin. You should be able to get a good shot on anyone jumping out the front or back."

Russell nodded and rose from the squat to a semi-crouch. "Yell when you're clear."

He ran to the side of the house, staying in the semi-crouch, and took up station behind a tree. He could see most of the front and probably three quarters of the back. The more he looked, though, the more he felt sorry for anyone who chose to jump out the back. If they did, they'd be hitting a sheer hill which plummeted about thirty feet. There was a back porch and a bit of a yard bordered by a small berm and then down through trees and brush. Not fun terrain. If they didn't die from the fall, they'd at least be broken in half.

Mickey snared his attention away from the hill. He shuffled toward the front door, moving like a lame dog, his right knee not quite flexing like it should. Leftover effects of a high school football injury. But he still had the quickness and grit. His face was a mask of determination. Lips tight, eyes narrow, left hand on the pump and right hand on the stock, finger on the guard vice the trigger.

When Mickey reached the front door he didn't hesitate. He aimed the shotgun at the lower end of the door where the hinge would be and fired. Instead of .00 buck, a slug tore through the door and knocked the bottom half clear of the frame. Mickey shifted his aim up and hit the top hinge with the second slug.

Russell scanned the windows. Still no shadows moving. No yelling either. All he could hear was the damn TV. Maybe it had been loud enough to mask the shots.

Mickey kicked the door in and disappeared out of sight. A few seconds passed. Some bitch on TV talked about taking a morning after pill. But nothing else. No more shots. No screams. No glass breaking. Nothing.

Russell licked his lips. Sweat broke out on his forehead and the back of his neck. The cool air met the perspiration, sending chills down to his heels. He tapped the stock of the shotgun.

There was a break in commercials. Peaceful silence drifted from the house for a second before it was filled with the pop of a gun discharging. Not Mickey's shotgun. Sounded more like a Glock.

The opening song of *Friends* started as Mickey answered the small shot with his own blast. Then another. There were no more pops after that. The band sang about being there for *you*.

Glass shattered to Russell's left. He pivoted and raised the shotgun. A man plunged from the second floor toward the ground feet first, long black hair flowing behind him. The *Friends* theme song ended as the guy hit the ground. Bone snapped, echoing around the side of the house, filling the vacuum of sound the music had left.

The guy screamed as his left leg went perpendicular to his body just above the ankle. No time to flail and cry and grasp at it, though. His momentum carried him into the berm at full speed, nailing it with his hip. His torso tumbled over and his

17

body followed, disappearing from view. Russell heard him as he bumped and rolled down the hill, screaming the whole way. On the TV the audience roared laughter.

Then there was a wet thud and the screams died. Russell edged to the berm and peeked over the top. About ten feet down, under the pale light of the moon, he found him. He'd broken his fall by ramming a huge tree trunk with his head. Blood gushed down the hill, looking like burnt oil leaking from a wrecked car. His left leg formed a backwards-L. His right twitched.

"Could use another hit," Russell said, barely a mumble, wishing he'd brought his pipe with him.

Another shotgun blast snatched his attention back toward the cabin. At least two people dead inside. Another one now part of a tree. Had to be it. At least he hoped it was. He needed another fix and that meant getting the hell out of here. But first he needed to get his fifty percent of whatever was inside. He prayed it was more than ten large.

The TV cut-off and silence once again enveloped him. A few seconds passed before Mickey yelled, "Russell, get your ass in here!"

Russell rubbed his mouth and jogged to the front, climbed a couple of concrete steps and entered, passing the kicked-in door. The first thing that hit him was the smell of spent gunpowder. Then the scent of blood and feces and spoiled food. He gagged and moved forward.

MANNY

Manny adjusted the elevation of his scope, accounting for the forty foot drop from his back deck into the valley below. He lined up the buck's head in the crosshairs. He didn't give a shit about damaging the rack. It was about the kill, not a trophy.

The wind gusted for a moment. Six knots from the west. He paused and adjusted his elbows, steadying the rifle on the bottom horizontal rail.

The wind died. Manny lined up the buck's head again. The moon shimmered in the glass-like surface of its right eye. It blinked and cocked its head toward Manny, the tips of its mighty antlers pointing at his face.

No way, he thought.

It looked right up the scope into Manny's soul. At least, it felt that way. There was wisdom in those eyes. Years of surviving the woods and its predators. Being the fastest. The strongest. None of that mattered, though. It never did in the end when someone had you in the crosshairs. What mattered then was the mercy of the shooter. A simple choice. Because bullets don't discriminate. They don't judge.

They equalize, Manny thought.

He eased off the trigger. Before he lowered the scope, the buck blinked and darted off into the woods.

"See you around."

Manny pushed up to his knees and then feet, joints cracking the whole way. Across the small valley, someone's television blasted *Seinfeld*. Probably those meth heads. They blast whatever's on all day and most of the night. At least they changed the channel from *Animal Planet*.

The noise wasn't a big deal to Manny. Nor the drugs he knew they were cooking. They didn't mess with him and he didn't mess them. If they wanted to cook meth and get high, more power to them. If they wanted to sell it, whatever. As long as they left him alone, he'd keep feeling that way.

Seinfeld ended and the valley was filled with silence again. Manny turned toward the sliding glass door, ready for a Rusty Nail and a microwave burrito, when a nine millimeter discharged. A distinctive little pop he'd heard many times in the past. He turned and lowered to one knee and tucked the rifled stock into his shoulder, barrel elevated five inches above the deck.

The theme song for *Friends* kicked on. Then a shotgun blast. Harder to hear over the music but still distinctive and much louder than the nine mil.

Manny started to reach into his pocket for his cell phone but paused. It was probably a shootout over drugs. No reason to interfere if they were going to wipe each other out. Plus he hated the Sheriff. A real asshole, that one. Not many people lived on the Loop. A few loners like him. Cookers. The rest of the places were empty until tourists flocked in for ski season and late-spring vacations. Some people free-camped down in the valley below, too. Not many in either case but enough to pique his concern for safety.

Another shotgun blast. Then another followed by a couple of pops. It was hard to discern live fire from echoes with all the damn singing.

Manny grabbed his cell phone and dialed 9-1-1.

"9-1-1, what's the emergency?" A woman's voice.

"Shots fired off Fool's Gold Loop. Near mile marker Four."

"Gunshots?"

Manny gritted his teeth. "Yes. Two types of guns. One nine millimeter handgun and at least one shotgun. Sounds like a twelve gauge. My bet is you have a shootout taking place."

"Can I get your name, Sir?"

Manny hung up.

The music cut-off.

Should go inside, Manny thought but didn't move. Instead, he remained in the kneeling position, rifle ready, listening.

GABE

Sheriff Gabe Clemons sighed as Tawny bobbed up and down on his cock. Or was it Tonya. Fuck it, it didn't matter.

He leaned back in his desk chair and gripped the arms tight. He clenched his ass cheeks and drove his dick up as she came down. The head hit the back of her throat but she didn't gag. No not Tawny. Tawny was a pro.

Literally.

Stanger brought her in two hours earlier. Busted her in the alley behind the 76 taking it up the ass from a trucker. He cuffed her for prostitution but let the trucker go. Had to be in San Diego by morning with a full load and Gabe didn't like interrupting commerce.

As for the hooker, well, Stanger knew Gabe had a soft spot for pros. Like any good deputy, he sought to keep the sheriff happy. If the boss is happy, everyone's happy. Gabe had trained him well.

"Faster." Gabe clenched a hand full of her oily black hair and push-lifted until she reached the desired speed. He straightened his legs and arched his back. The next time she came down, he held her head there, even pushed it down more. He felt the tightness of her throat on the head. Then he shot. "Ahhh."

Tawny being the pro she was, let it flow and swallowed everything he gave her. After a few more seconds, Gabe released his death grip on her hair and allowed her to extract him from her mouth. She rocked back, still on her knees, and wiped slobber from her chin.

"That was mighty fine." Gabe pushed up from his leather chair and hiked his pants up. "Mighty fine indeed."

"So no jail time, right?" Tawny had the voice of a crippled mouse; squeaky and broken.

Gabe nodded and buckled his belt. He turned and lifted the towel he'd been sitting on from the chair and tossed it in the corner next to his coat rack. It joined three or four others.

"Yep, you earned your get out of jail card." Gabe extended his hand and helped her to her feet. Tawny straightened her tight little mini skirt and ran her hands through her hair. She wasn't a bad looking hooker. A little rough on the eyes. Crow's feet. Worn lips. A second chin starting to dangle. But the tits were nice and fake and the ass round and firm. Not bad at all. "Feel free to come see me anytime."

Tawny chuckled. "Looking for a kickback?"

"A kickback implies you'll get to keep doing what you do for money."

Tawny's smile faded. "What the hell are you saying?"

"Stanger," Gabe said, looking past Tawny to the door.

A moment later, it opened and his fat young deputy stepped through. "Yes, Sheriff?"

"Hundred dollar fine for Miss Tawny here."

"You got it."

"Hundred dollars?" Tawny's broken mouse squeak of a voice shot up an octave or two. "You said I earned my get out of jail free card."

"I said you earned your get out of jail card. Rather than a night in jail and a date with the judge, I've reduced your penalty to a fine and a blowjob. Pay it and you're free to go."

"That's bullshit."

"I can make it two hundred dollars." Gabe stepped close and leaned into her ear. "And Stanger will get to fuck you for free."

Tawny shook her head but said nothing.

"You don't fuck for money anymore in my town. Got that? You turn tricks, do it somewhere else."

"What'd I do?"

"I just said you got caught fucking for money in my town. I'm pretty fair when it comes down to it. You break the law and don't get caught, well, there's not much I can do about that. But when you're dumb enough to end up in the back of one of my cruisers, I've got to put you out of business. That's why the good citizens of Tallwood voted for me. Now pay the fine and get the fuck out of here."

Stanger took Tawny by the arm and walked her out the door. As she left, Gabe noticed her shoulders hitch up and down and heard the first few soft cries. Then she was down the hall and out of eye and ear shot.

Gabe smiled and swaggered over to the other side of the office. He fired up the Bose Wave CD player he'd bought on eBay and slid in the Misfits *Earth A.D.* A couple of clicks and *Green Hell* roared over the speakers. Gabe went into full air guitar mode, head banging and screaming Glenn Danzig's lyrics at the top of his lungs.

Half-way through the song, Gabe quit singing and started howling like a wolf at the moon. He was on his third howl when a hand tapped his shoulder. Gabe spun and fired a left jab, hitting Stanger in the forehead. His right hand had his sidearm drawn and leveled at his deputy a second later.

Stanger threw up his hands and said, "Whoa, whoa, whoa."

Gabe's jaw tightened. He reached behind him and switch off the gnashing punk rock. "Damn it, I told you not to sneak up on me when I'm in my zone."

"Shit, sorry, Sheriff." Stanger rubbed his forehead. "Just wanted to let you know she paid the freight. I told Lyle to take her out to the town line."

Gabe nodded. "How's the head?"

Stanger quit rubbing. "Hurts like a bitch."

"Ah, it can't be that bad." Gabe chuckled and holstered his sidearm and removed his gun belt and hung it on the coat rack and moved back around his desk and sat down. "Bet my hand hurts more. You've got one fucking solid melon."

Stanger chuckled albeit weakly.

Gabe motioned at the chair across from him. "Have a seat."

Stanger did. Gabe opened the top right drawer of his desk and pulled out a bottle of Wild Turkey. He set two highball glasses next to it. He poured two fingers worth in each and pushed one across to his deputy.

"Drink up." Gabe reclined back and sipped his. "You did good work tonight."

Stanger sighed, his jowls jiggling. "Wasn't exactly hard." He drank half the glass. "No pun intended."

"Well, you landed the town another hundred dollars and put a whore out of business. Not too bad in my book."

Stanger shrugged and polished off the Turkey. Gabe offered him the bottle. He took it and refilled his glass.

"Something bothering you, Stanger?"

"Nah."

Gabe smirked. "You don't like that I used the whore and then kicked her out, do you?"

"Nailing some whore don't bother me none—"

"But taking her money and forcing her out of town does."

"Just seems like we're taking the court out of the process is all. We've been doing that a lot lately."

Gabe nodded and refilled his glass. "You're right. I am taking the court out of the process. Where I can. Do you know why?"

"Make it easier. Get it over and done with."

"You could say that. Here's something else, though. How much tax payer money would have been spent on Miss Tawny if we were to book her and await the judge? It'd take a couple of days to get to the courthouse based on the schedule. You know she'd have to have a court appointed attorney. More tax payer money down the drain. And let's not forget meals, toiletries, and the cost in man-hours to ensure a guard was here twenty-four, seven."

Stanger took a sip. "I see your point."

"We made a hundred dollar profit, minus the money on gas you spent to bring her here and for Lyle to take her out past the town line. It only took a couple of man-hours. Most importantly, we won't have a repeat offender on our hands, sucking even more tax payer money down the jizz hole. Pun intended."

Stanger laughed. "Was it good?"

"Better than my cold right hand."

They both laughed and refilled their glasses. About a quarter remained in the bottle now. Gabe rubbed his eyes, ready to call it a night soon. He sipped and rested the glass on his stomach.

"You think she'll stay out of Tallwood?" Stanger said.

"If she's got half a brain she will. Not that I've got anything against a woman making money with her snatch. I mean there's nothing wrong at all with a nice little private operation. If she had a house and set it up where she had personal clients, no problem. Hell I'd probably be her Wednesday night regular. But fucking truckers for ten bucks at *Lou's Stop and Pump* or behind the 76 isn't the way to conduct business. She steps foot in Tallwood again, I'll take more than a hundred out of her ass."

"Why don't we go round up the meth cookers and show them the polite door as well?"

"Got to catch them first."

"Shit, we know where they are." Stanger leaned forward. "I can point out two trailers and four cabins in this town where meth is being cooked or bagged for distribution."

"I hear you." Gabe set the empty glass down and rested his elbows on the desk. "But we're not vigilantes. We catch a hooker fucking in a parking lot, we take care of it our way. But we catch her in the act first. We catch a dealer slinging or some dickwad cooking, we take care of it our way. We don't knock doors down on hunches or what some angry neighbor says."

Stanger finished off his Turkey and belched. "Like we took care of that little shit Wheezy."

Gabe pointed his finger at Stanger and flexed his thumb like it was a gun. "Bingo. Wheezy ain't been back since."

"What if we find a way to draw them out? Say we put them in a situation where they just happen to have product on them and we just happen to catch them?"

Gabe smirked and poured the last of the Turkey in his glass. He rocked back and lifted his feet onto the desk, crossing one polished boot over the other.

"Well, if something like that were to happen, it would have to be planned carefully so as not to turn the criminal into a victim or place any of our people in a possibly violent confrontation."

Stanger nodded. "Don't roll up on the meth house with one armed deputy."

"And don't roll up on the meth house with an army and pretend like you're just passing by and heard something out of the ordinary."

"I understand, Sheriff."

Gabe drained the glass and pointed it at Stanger. "You're starting to think about this shit the right way. You put your mind to it and find me a way to nail some of these meth cookers, and we'll make them gone. Permanently."

"Fucking A."

Gabe leaned forward and set the glass to the side and rested his elbows on a blotter covered in doodles. He sighed heavily. "Well, all talking aside, I think I'm about spent for the night."

"Yeah, me, too." Stanger stood and rolled his neck. It popped in about five places. "Been a long one."

"Who's got the duty tonight with Lyle?"

"Pronger."

Gabe nodded. "On your way out, call Lyle and tell him to radio me when Miss Tawny is dropped off. No calls after that unless the town's burning or something."

"Roger that."

Stanger tipped his cap and turned and took two steps when static burst over his radio. No voice followed, though. He stopped and turned back to Gabe.

Gabe shrugged. "Maybe Lyle sat on his and keyed it by accident."

"Yeah, probably."

Gabe's radio burst next. His eyebrows narrowed as he picked it up and keyed it. "Lyle, is that you trying to reach one of us?"

"Sorry, Sheriff, it's Dispatch. I hit the wrong number the first time."

"Debbie, damn it, I'm down the hall. You don't have to call me on the radio when I'm in the office."

"Yes, Sheriff. I didn't know if you were...indisposed."

Gabe eyed Stanger. "Debbie knows?"

A grin a fox would be proud of spread across Stanger's mouth. "Shit, everyone knows."

Gabe didn't like that. "One of you guys run your mouth?"

"Nope. I think she heard through the door a few times. Did the math."

Well, there was nothing to be done about that. Debbie hadn't said anything or even dropped a hint she knew about his tastes. That said something about her. Loyal. Dutiful.

"Sheriff?" Debbie's voice broke over the radio again.

Gabe blinked, remembering she'd called. "It's just me and Stanger. Come on down."

"Wonder what's up?" Stanger said.

Gabe had half a response out when the door flew open and Debbie ran in. She huffed and puffed. Her ample breasts rose and fell against a khaki button down. Her face, flushed. Eyes wide. Sweat dotted her forehead. She was pushing forty but was still in good shape. The run down the hall didn't have this effect on her. Something else had excited her to the point of hyperventilating.

"Jesus, Debbie, what is it?" Gabe started around the desk.

"Shootout."

"What?" Gabe and Stanger said at the same time.

"Shootout." She took a deep breath and spoke as she exhaled. "9-1-1 call just came in. Several shots fired up off Fool's Gold Loop."

Stanger's head snapped to Gabe. "Cookers up in one of those cabins."

Gabe held up a hand. "Who made the call, Debbie?"

"Anonymous male. But they said it sounded like several shotgun blasts and a handgun."

"Did he say what kind of handgun?"

"Nine millimeter."

Gabe turned to Stanger. "Manny Lopez."

"How do you know?"

"Because Manny's a former Marine sniper. Who else up on the Loop could pick out a shotgun and a nine mil? Hell, who else is on the Loop this time of year other than Manny and free-campers?"

"Good point. Why didn't he just give his name?"

"Because he's a paranoid fuck who hates government. It

probably took him ten minutes to talk himself into making the call." Gabe turned back to Debbie. Her breathing had slowed some. "Did he say where on the Loop?"

"Said it sounded like it came from around mile marker Four."

"The old Robertson place," Stanger said. "Definitely cookers. Young punks. Seen them around town. One of them inherited the cabin or some shit like that."

Gabe placed his hands on his hips, nodding. "Good job, Debbie. Go back out and radio Lyle. Tell him to meet us at the bottom of the Loop."

"Okay, Sheriff." She headed for the door, stopped, and turned back around. "Should I send emergency services?"

"Not yet. We'll check it out first. Don't want a couple of EMTs getting shot."

She half-smiled and left.

"Stanger, get Pronger and Betts over there."

"Want the Armory opened?"

"No. Shotguns and sidearms only. I doubt there'll be anyone shooting by the time we get there."

"Just the injured and the dead."

"Just the dead."

Stanger's eyes opened a few centimeters beyond normal.

Gabe winked. "We'll make these cookers go away permanently. Right?"

Stanger's face lit up. "Right."

"Well, let's get moving then." Gabe grabbed his gun belt from the coat rack. "You're driving."

RUSSELL

Russell found a living room on the left. Mickey stood in front of the TV, back to him, shoulders rising and falling on heavy breaths. Behind him, a bunch of Chinese food cartons left out on a cable-spool coffee table.

"Mickey."

No response.

"Mickey." Russell almost yelled his name.

Mickey turned. The front of his face and shirt were splattered with blood. His eyes were wide but still sharp.

Mickey pointed at his ear. "Fucking nearly deaf from the shots and fucking TV."

Russell nodded.

"Did you get the asshole who jumped out the window?" Mickey yelled every word.

Russell didn't feel like screaming the story of what happened so Mickey could hear it. Instead, he nodded some more and looked around the room. It was small, dominated by the big LCD TV on the far wall and cable-spool coffee table. Two recliners, one maroon and the other emerald, sat across from the LCD. No couch or loveseat. Budweiser cans littered a mildewed hardwood floor.

"The other two were upstairs hiding." Mickey's voice wasn't as loud now. "I think we caught them sleeping."

"How could they sleep with the TV?"

"Got me? All I know is they were in their bedrooms. First guy tried to get me on the stairwell. Second guy dove out the window before I could blast him. Last guy was hiding in the shower with a knife of all things."

"And the upstairs is clear?"

"Fuck yeah it is."

"So what's left?" Russell shifted, glancing down a hallway,

shotgun at hip level.

"Besides here and the kitchen, there's a half-bath and the garage where they do the cooking."

"Did you check the garage?"

"Nah. Was waiting for you. Figure we'd check it out together. That way, whatever we find, you can't say I gypped you."

"No money upstairs?"

"Nope. So let's check the garage already."

Mickey moved past him and turned down the hallway toward the garage. He carried the shotgun at his side barrel down while he wiped blood from his face with his other hand. Russell followed, gun still at his hip.

They reached a door at the end of the hallway. Mickey stopped and turned to him. "Ready?"

"You sure this is the garage?"

"Yeah."

"How do you know?"

"You can tell from the layout. Outside, the garage is on this side. This the only door. So on the other side is the garage."

Russell raised the shotgun and pointed it at the door. "After you."

Mickey smirked and grabbed the knob and twisted it. Russell expected him to ease the door open in case someone was waiting on the other side. Instead, Mickey threw it open without a care in the world.

The sudden movement surprised Russell and he ducked back away from the frame. He didn't know what to expect. Gun shots. Mickey's chest exploding in red mushrooms. Something. But what he got was a vacuum of silence which was quickly filled with Mickey's laughter.

"Pussy," Mickey said.

Russell dry swallowed and peeked around the frame. The garage was lit by several hanging workshop lights. Two long tables sat in the middle, holding the equipment of the trade: flasks, piping, burners, gas masks, and so forth. At the end of the table closest to them was a clear plastic box filled with glass, bagged and ready for distribution.

Mickey whistled and walked over to the box and picked up a baggie. "The quality is shit but we should make some decent money unloading it. More than enough to make a few payments on your ma's treatment, right?"

"Yeah."

Mickey dropped the baggie back in the tray. "We'll leave the equipment. It's pretty old and nasty shit. Probably stole it from their old high school."

Russell joined him at the tray. He grabbed a baggie and opened it and shook the contents on the table. With the butt of the shotgun, he smashed the crystal. Then he grabbed a pinch of coarse dust and snorted it up his right nostril.

"Need it that bad, huh?" Mickey shook his head.

"I should have brought my pipe." Russell snorted a pinch up the left nostril and shook his head and wiped his nose with the back of his hand. His body started to relax almost right away.

"How is it?"

"Not bad."

"Bullshit." Mickey grabbed a pinch and snorted. He waited a few moments. "Remember that episode of *Seinfeld* when the dentist became a Jew so he could joke about Jews?"

"Yeah." Russell took one more hit, laughing. "Jerry was offended as a comedian."

"Right. And the dentist wasn't really a Jew. He was pretending to be. But what he really was, was a fucking poser." Mickey pointed at the dust. "That's what this shit is. A fucking poser."

"It's just weak." Russell looked around the room at the equipment. "They were still getting the technique down."

"Whatever. This shit is only good for dregs and lowlifes. We'll unload it in Shit Town. Sell it cheap and move it quick."

Russell turned in a slow circle, taking in the rest of the garage.

"What the hell you doing?"

"Seeing if they have a stash." Russell moved to a set of shelves on the other side. They were filled with cardboard boxes and plastic bins. He set the shotgun on the concrete floor and pulled a box from the bottom shelf.

"I doubt they stashed the money in a box."

Russell opened it. Old Christmas decorations. He dug through it anyway. "Won't know until you check. Unless you got a better idea where it's at."

"No." Mickey grabbed a box and started digging through. "Got no clue."

Tap, tap, tap.

Russell froze, hands in a box full of baby clothes. Maybe it was whatever Mickey was pawing through.

Tap, tap, tap.

This time Mickey froze. "Did you hear that?"

"Yeah."

"It wasn't you?"

"No."

Tap, tap, tap.

Russell and Mickey grabbed their shotguns and rose. They stood there, listening. Russell cocked his head, hoping he could zero in on where the sound had come from. He wasn't sure if it had been inside or out.

Tap, tap, tap.

Inside.

Mickey motioned with his head toward the rear of the garage. Russell nodded. It sounded like it was coming from the back wall. Maybe a rat or something.

He took a step toward the sound. Then another. One foot over the other. The shotgun raised and he gazed down the barrel. He half expected a rat to scurry out from under the pile of scrap wood tucked in the back corner.

Tap, tap, tap.

Mickey followed behind him, breathing slow and shallow. Russell licked his lips. He was thankful he'd taken a few hits, even if it was shitty product.

Tap, tap, tap.

Russell reached a storage locker and leaned in close. The sound didn't come from within. He looked up, hoping he'd see a rodent on top moving around. No such luck. But he did see half a wall.

The locker had been pushed up against the back wall of the garage. Except the back wall only ran half way behind the locker. Looking from left to right, there was wall and then a sharp ninety degree corner. The back of the garage was actually deeper than it first appeared.

Russell moved around the side. Hidden from view behind it was a door, perpendicular to the back of the locker.

"Cleaning gear room," Mickey said, his voice a tight whisper. "Or maybe a laundry room."

Tap, tap, tap.

The sound was definitely coming from the other side of the hidden door. Russell swallowed and stepped closer. He glanced at Mickey, who nodded. Then he reached out and gripped the knob. He gave a slight twist. It moved. Not locked.

He twisted it all the way and threw the door open and stepped aside and Mickey moved forward.

"Get your fucking hands in the air!" Mickey stood in the doorframe.

Russell wondered why Mickey didn't just blow whoever it was away. Then he peeked over his shoulder and realized. A long haired white dude sat at a card table piled high with glass. Mickey didn't want to get blood on the product.

It only took Russell another moment to see an open gym bag on the floor at the dude's feet. Inside, rolls of tens and twenties filled it to the zipper and starting to spill out. The stash.

Russell pushed past Mickey and raised his shotgun. "Did you fucking hear him, man? Get your fucking hands in the air."

The dude picked up a small sledge hammer and tap, tap, tapped a handful of meth into dust. Then he swept it into a small dustpan and dumped it in a Tupperware bowl.

Russell's eyes widened. The bowl was completely full of dust and rose above the edge in a rounded summit. He glanced at Mickey, who shrugged.

The dude giggled. Not in a funny way. In an insane way. At least, that's what Russell thought. Then they guy grabbed more glass and tap, tap, tapped and swept it into the bowl.

"Hey, buddy," Mickey said. "What the fuck are you doing?"

The dude stopped and lifted his head. His eyes were bloodshot behind wire-rimmed glasses. He was young, probably no older than nineteen or twenty. A big grin spread across his face.

Russell swallowed, suddenly nervous. Something wasn't just off with this guy. He was completely over the edge. Bugfuck crazy. And bugfuck crazy and meth didn't go well together.

"I'm making dinner," the dude said. His voice was ragged and strained.

Mickey motioned at the bowl overflowing with dust with the barrel. "That's a big dinner."

The dude shrugged. "Big appetites require big portions." He giggled. "Big portions."

Mickey's left eyebrow arched up and shifted to Russell. Now Russell shrugged, not liking this. It was too...weird.

"You want to kill yourself, I'll oblige," Mickey said. "Just step away from the glass and cash and I'll end you right now."

"Got to feed it first." The dude turned back to the glass. He took the hammer and tap, tap, tapped.

"It?" Russell said.

"It'll be up soon. It'll be hungry. Jonesing like you wouldn't believe. The others thought we'd be good through the rest of the cook. But I know better. It'll be up and ready for more."

"What the fuck are you talking about?" Mickey said and inched closer.

"You wait too long, it gets angry. I mean rip your arms out angry." Tap, tap, tap. Sweep. "Just ask Jimmy." The dude giggled again. "Actually, you can't ask Jimmy."

"He one of the ones I blew away upstairs?"

"What? Uh, no." Tap, tap, tap. Sweep. "Jimmy's dead. Took too long to feed the need. Didn't feed it enough. Got used to the dose. Needed more. But we didn't know. And Jimmygot got. So we figure we need to kill it. But we need to get close and if it's up and hungry, need a meal ready to satiate it. Or we end up like Jimmy. Unless we burn the place down.

Need to finish the cook first."

Mickey pressed the barrel against the dude's head. "Get up you crazy fuck and back away from the table. Now."

The dude shook his head. "Got to feed the need." Tap, tap, tap. Instead of a sweep, the dude bent down and snorted damn near a hand full of powder. He shivered and laughed and wiped his nose with the back of his hand. "Can't feed it until I get fed, too, you know what I'm saying? Can't face it without a taste."

"Face what?" Russell said.

"Fuck it," Mickey said. "This dude if fucking cracked. Grab the stash and I'll blow him away. Fuck the meth that's left in here."

"Sure." Russell grabbed the bag of cash and zipped it closed. "Sure thing."

Mickey started to squeeze the trigger when the dude pushed away from the table and rose. The sudden movement caused both of them to step back.

"Sit your ass back down." Mickey regained the step he'd surrendered.

"No can do, man." The dude checked his watch. "Only got a few minutes left and I got to get the right amount. If it ain't the right amount, might as well not give it any at all."

The dude lifted the bowl of dust, turning it slowly in his hand, surveying the mound. Then he gently set it on a scale. He clapped. "Nailed it."

"Come on, Mickey." Russell scratched his neck. "Do this guy and let's get the fuck out of here. Cops could be on their way."

"True that." Mickey never took his eyes off the dude. "Snort one more noseful now cuz it's your last."

The dude lifted the bowl. "You need to step aside. I have to deliver this right now."

Mickey laughed. "Shit son, you're done. Might as well set it down and close your eyes."

The dude took a step toward Mickey as if to push by him. Mickey pushed the barrel into the dude's cheek.

"Ain't you full of energy all the sudden?"

"I got to deliver—"

"The product. I got that part."

"If it ain't there when it wakes up—"

"It gets angry, whatever the fuck it is. Got that part, too. Got it all, including you're high and crazy. None of it matters, though. I'm done talking to you."

"It'll wake up any—"

"Hush now and it'll be over in a sec."

Something roared. Loud. Reverberating off the walls from somewhere down. Somewhere below them.

MANNY

Manny knelt, listening, waiting for more gunshots or the sound of cop sirens. Neither came. Not yet at least.

Pines creaked in the slight wind. A small animal sprinted across pine needles and dry twigs, rustling and snapping until it faded around a property to the left. A fire crackled somewhere down in the valley.

An ungodly roar ripped through the Loop. Manny didn't jump but would readily admit it induced a shiver or two. He'd heard something similar the last couple of weeks. Here and there. Figured it was just something on *Animal Planet* being broadcasted at an unbearable volume. Not now, though. No, this was real and here. It sure as hell wasn't any animal either. At least not one he recognized. Manny knew the animals in this region pretty well. Whatever made that noise was foreign.

It roared again. He blinked and shook his head. There was something familiar in the tenor of it. He'd heard it before. Not around here but definitely before.

Fallujah, Manny thought. The IED that took his spotter's leg and most of his torso. Chris flopped in his blood as Manny held his hand, whimpering. Then Chris roared. Not screamed. Roared. Not as loud as the one Manny just heard. Nowhere near the same sound. But the same tenor? Yes. The same anguish and fury and desperation. It dissolved into a final gasp and Chris died.

Manny touched his right side where the shrapnel had shredded his oblique. Mostly scar tissue now. The only wound he suffered that day. Chris had taken the blunt of the explosion and paid the ultimate price.

Strange it was a roar and not a gunshot that sent him diving into the past. Then again was it? It seemed to happen that way often enough. He heard gunshots from time to time on the Loop. Hunters in and out of season. No flashbacks then. Ever. No, it was the odd things he didn't expect that triggered the memories. The certain way a car's exhaust smelled on a hot day. Similar to a HUMVEE burning fuel as it raced to help a bombed-out buddy. The flavor of canned ravioli, so similar to the way the MREs in the field tasted. The hot sun beating down on his face on a dry summer day. Not desert like but enough to remind him of those early mornings in country before the anvil of Vulcan really heated up. A guy laughing in the grocery story. Eerily similar to Chris's. So much so Manny forgot where he was for a second or two.

Now this.

Another roar snapped Manny out of the past and back into the present.

What the hell could it be? Did he really want to find out?

Just go inside, he thought. *Go inside and watch* Sportscenter *and leave this alone. Your time protecting people is over.*

No, he'd wait. Wait until he heard or saw the cops. Then he'd surrender the watch. He could live with himself then.

GABE

"Run the plates," Gabe said.

Stanger complied, punching in the Ford's license plate number. It sat parked at the foot of the long driveway heading up toward the old Robertson place. It looked familiar but in the dark, it could be any local shitkicker's.

Gabe hummed "Green Hell" and tapped his thigh. He glanced in the side view mirror. Lyle's car was parked behind them. The deputy sat there, picking his nose. Gabe shook his head a looked away. Pronger and Betts hadn't showed up yet. Betts was off duty at home. Pronger had to pick him up. But they should've been there by now.

"Any bets on whether Betts was passed out drunk?" Gabe said.

"I'd be an idiot to take that bet."

Yes, you would, Gabe thought.

They'd just pulled up and started to swing in the driveway when they noticed the truck parked off to the side. Gabe had considered passing it by but the place was quiet. No gunshots. No screams. None of the stuff you'd expect from a shootout. Maybe they were all dead.

Or maybe there wasn't a shootout, he thought. Maybe Manny Lopez had heard someone's cranked-up television and had a flashback.

Maybe.

Hell, the more he thought about it the more likely it was.

Stanger cleared his throat. "Here we go. Truck's registered to Mickey Gannon."

"That little shit? One who runs with Russell O'Brien?"

"That's the one. Meth pushers, too."

"But this isn't their base of operations."

"Nope. Haven't figured out where they cook. Then again

haven't really tried. They're pros. The assholes in the cabin are rookies, from what I hear."

I guess we had a shootout after all. "So that came to wipe out the new competition."

"Appears that way."

Tires crunched gravel. Gabe looked out his window to see Pronger's puffy face smiling at him. He rolled down the window.

"Hey, Sheriff."

"Pronger." Gabe saw Betts slumped over in the passenger seat. A long string of drool dangled down to his chest. "Not exactly fit for duty, is he?"

"He'll be all right." Pronger slapped Betts's chest. "Wake up, asshole."

Betts's head shot up and his eyes bolted open. "Fuck, man." Then he saw Gabe. "Oh, shit. Sorry, Sheriff. Just catching more shuteye. I'm good to go."

"You sure?"

"Hell, yes. I wouldn't miss this."

Gabe shook his head. "Fine then. Here's the pla—"

A roar cut him off.

"What the fuck was that?" Betts nearly screamed.

"Just a damn bear," Pronger said.

Gabe didn't think it was a bear. No bear he ever heard at least. And he'd shot a couple of bears in his life.

"Think we should still head up there?" Stanger said.

"You pussing out on me?"

"Nah. Just didn't sound right—"

The roar came again. Then more in rapid succession.

Gabe rubbed his mouth. "That ain't a bear."

RUSSELL

Russell jumped at the sound of the roar and lost his grip on the shotgun. It slipped from his fingers and hit the concrete floor, discharging a round of buckshot that tore through the side of a dryer. The concussion inside the small space caused almost complete deafness. But he heard the roar again. Muffled. And this time he felt it, vibrating the floor underneath his feet.

"What the fuck is that?" Mickey shouted.

Russell scooped up the shotgun. "I don't know but let's get out of here."

"What is th—" Mickey's words stuck somewhere in his throat when he turned and found the dude gone. He spun around. "Where the fuck did he go?"

Russell stared where the dude had been standing. Gone with his bowl of powder. "I don't know."

"What do you mean you don't know?"

"I was picking up the shotgun." Russell pointed at Mickey. "How did you lose sight of him?"

"I ducked when your jumpy ass dropped the gun." Mickey kicked the table. "Shit."

Another roar.

"Christ, what the hell is that?" Russell said, rubbing his face.

"I don't know but it ain't my main concern right now."

"He knows our faces, man. We need to find him."

"Well fucking duh."

Mickey hustled out of the room. Russell slung the bag of cash over his shoulder and followed. Across from them was another open door leading outside. The wind had picked up. Branches swayed and creaked.

"Oh, Christ." Russell stopped just outside and looked around at the night. "He's gone, man. He's fucking gone."

"He can't be that far. We can still get him."

"We don't have time."

"We're fine."

"Should have just shot him. He played crazy to fool us. Fuck. We're so fucked. He knows our faces. Damn it, he knows what we look like."

"Shut up. We can probably hear him running if you quit freaking out and listen. Feel me?"

"But I can barely hear."

"It's getting better right?"

"Sort of."

"And it's quiet out. So stand still and listen as best you can."

Russell took hard, fast breaths, trying to calm his hammering heart down. "Yeah, yeah it's pretty quiet out."

"Right. So relax and listen."

Russell did as best he could. He cocked his head as a wind gust kicked up and rustled the nearby trees. An owl hooted somewhere in the distance.

Then he heard metal clinking. Fast. Like someone trying to unlock a gate in a hurry.

"Hear that?" Mickey said.

"Yeah."

"Coming from around back."

They headed toward the rear of the cabin, taking it slow, shotguns raised. The closer they got, the louder the noise grew.

Another roar.

Both stopped.

"I think it came from behind the house," Russell said.

"Nah, more like the other side. Probably down the hill. Maybe a bear."

"That don't sound like any bear I've ever heard."

"And how many bears have you heard?"

Russell shrugged and adjusted the bag's strap digging into his neck.

"Then shut the fuck up and keep moving unless you want to end up in a nice cozy cell with a couple of wetbacks cornholing you."

Russell pushed himself forward. The metal noise resumed. Clink, clink, clink. Then a dragging sound.

The roar came again, reverberating off the trees.

"Mickey, it's coming from in the house."

"Fuck you say."

"I'm telling you whatever made that sound is in the house."

"I didn't see any bear in the house. I think I would have noticed."

"Maybe—"

"I got it right here." The voice of the dude.

Mickey held a finger against his lips. He motioned for Russell to move to the side of the house. Russell shook his head. Mickey pointed the shotgun at him and mouthed, *Now.*

Russell licked his lips and pressed his back against the side of the cabin. He inched down toward the corner, feet trampling through a bed of dead flowers. Mickey remained a few feet back and to his right.

"Just be cool," the dude said. More metal dragging. "And don't tear my arms off, please."

Another roar.

Russell froze, the shotgun shaking in his hands.

"I said be cool," the dude said. "I got it right here." Clink, clink. "It'll be over soon." Drag. "We'll finish the cook and then burn down the house with you in it." Giggle.

Russell reached the corner of the cabin and paused. Mickey pointed at his own eyes with his right index and middle fingers and then motioned with his hand: *look around the corner*. Russell shook his head as another roar rose up. It was almost as loud as the blast from when he dropped the shotgun. Worse, actually. Shriller. Ear piercing.

Mickey motioned with the shotgun: *fucking check around the corner*.

Russell swallowed and inched forward and peeked around the corner. The dude knelt before a cellar door, fumbling with padlocks and pulling chains. Big, thick chains.

He's going to let whatever the fuck it is out, Russell thought as he ducked away. He turned to Mickey and waved him over.

"What'd you see?" Mickey whispered.

"There's a cellar door. That crazy bastard is unlocking a bunch of chains keeping it closed."

"What?"

"See for yourself. Big fucking chains. Circus-type."

Mickey leaned and peeked and then pulled back. "What the hell—"

A roar cut him off.

"I think he's going to let out whatever's in the cellar," Russell said. "Let's get the fuck out of here."

"We can't let him go."

"By the way it sounds, when he opens that door what's down there is going to take care of him for us."

Mickey nibbled on his bottom lip. "Doesn't make any sense."

"No shit."

"I mean why would he want to let a pissed-off bear out?"

Russell started to say he didn't know when he thought about the big bowl of meth. "Fuck, Mickey, the bear's hooked."

"What?"

"The bowl. The powder. Time to feed the need."

"Oh, shit." Mickey rubbed his forehead. "They got a fucking bear hooked for fun."

Another roar.

"Think that's why they had the TV so loud," Russell said. "Drown it out between meals."

Mickey shook his head. "Let's ice this idiot before it gets free."

He stepped around the corner. Russell straightened the bag of cash behind his back and followed.

"Back the fuck away from the door," Mickey said.

The dude's head shot up from the chains. "Hey man, I'm almost done here, okay?"

"What's down there?" Russell said.

The dude turned back to the chains. "No time to talk. If it doesn't get the product—"

Mickey fired. Buckshot ripped through the dude's arm and shoulder and face. Most of his head disappeared in a cloud of flesh and blood. His body pitched sideways, twitching.

The thing in the cellar roared. Russell backed away but Mickey checked him with his hand. "We need to get those chains back on."

The roar turned into something else. Painful. Desperate. Not a cry, though. No, it still had a vicious cut to it.

"Fuck that." Russell walked past the twitching dude on his way around the house. The bowl of powder was tipped over next to him, half-soaked in blood.

"Russell, damn it, get back here."

Russell stopped and turned around. "We've wasted too much time and I'm not going to be here when a junky bear breaks out of that cellar. Let the cops deal with it."

Mickey looked down at the cellar door and the last chain holding it in place and then back to Russell. "Yeah, you right."

The cellar door burst up. The wood cracked and split around the remaining chain. Then another hit in rapid succession. Large splinters ripped the air. One final hit and most of the door blew up and away from the hinges. Mickey shielded his face with his arm and backpedaled. Russell just watched, dumbfounded by the sudden destruction.

Then something reached up out of the darkness of the cellar. A hand. A brown furry hand. Not a paw. Not a claw. But five enormous digits. Like a gorilla's only bigger. They wrapped around the last remaining chain. The thing roared and yanked down and the thick circus chain snapped and disappeared out of sight. The shotgun fell from Russell's hands again. Not out of fear. This time, out of total disbelief.

"What the fuck?" Mickey said.

"Get away from there."

"What the fuck was that?"

"A bear."

"Wasn't no bear."

Russell stopped arguing when he heard sniffing. The damn thing was sniffing the air. Then his eyes darted to the bowl of dust, tipped on its side, its content on the ground and saturated with blood.

"Micky, get the fuck—"

His voice was cut-off by a roar and heavy pounding

footsteps. The thing sprung out of the cellar and had Mickey in its grasp before he could fire another round. Russell could do nothing but stare.

An ape. No, it was too big to be an ape. The thing towered over Mickey. It was covered in rich brown fur, not black like a gorilla or orange like an orangutan. No, this thing was colored like a damn grizzly. But it sure as hell wasn't a grizzly.

Fucking Bigfoot, Russell thought.

The thing lifted Mickey in the air so he was eye level with it. Then it unleashed the loudest roar yet. Triumphant. Russell winced as it pierced his eardrums. It was soon outdone by Mickey's screams.

Russell watched as it ripped Mickey's arms out at the shoulder. He dropped to the ground, kicking and wailing, blood jutting in all directions as Bigfoot stood over him, arms firmly in its grasp still. Then it lifted its right foot and stomped down on his head and his screams stopped for good.

Bigfoot dropped the arms and turned and fell to its knees and scooped as much of the powder into its hands as it could and brought it to its nose and snorted and snorted until its hands were empty. It shuddered and sighed and Russell, for a moment, understood how it felt. Then it picked up another handful and repeated the process. When it was gone, it licked its fingers and palms clean.

Then it started to emit a low, wheezing sound. It took Russell a moment to realize the thing was crying. And again, Russell understood how it felt.

Red and blue lights flashed in the corner of his eyes. He turned. Several Sheriff's cars drove up toward the cabin.

"Fuck me," Russell said and started to reach for his shotgun.

Too loud.

Bigfoot's head snapped toward him. The eyes, bloodshot and wild, fixed on him like a heat-seeking missile. Its leather-like face dotted here and there with blood and meth.

"Oh, shit." He backed away from the gun.

To his right, tires crunched gravel and brakes squeaked. In front of him, Bigfoot rose and turned so that its massive frame faced Russell. But it really wasn't massive. Russell could see that now. Still muscular but withered away, too. All that fur hanging on it like baggy clothes. The body of a junky.

It tilted its hairy head back and sniffed the air. Then it lowered its head and resumed its lock on him.

"Fuck me."

Doors opened and shut. People spoke but Russell couldn't make out what they said. He heard a few shotguns pump.

Across from him, Bigfoot flexed its thighs as if ready to jump. Twenty or so feet separated them and Russell didn't doubt the thing could probably cover the distance in a single bound.

That didn't stop him. He spun and took off, legs churning like a runaway locomotive. He avoided the berm and found a less extreme decline and managed to keep his feet at a full sprint. Branches smacked his arms and legs and cheeks. None of them slowed him down.

Behind him, he didn't hear footsteps. Instead, Russell heard panicked yells and another roar. Then gunshots.

Russell kept running, the sound of violence echoing around him.

MANNY

Roar after roar. No screams though. If he'd heard a scream, Manny would stop watching and start toward the menacing sounds. He could only resist so long before the old reflexes kicked in and a scream would shatter that resistance to pieces. Hell, he was sweating already. Perspiration dotted his forehead. He could feel wet rings under his arms. It took a great deal of energy to do nothing.

The sniper training paid off in cases like this. Plenty of times he'd witnessed incidents he could have easily intervened in. But he'd maintained focus, waiting for the perfect moment to strike. He allowed regular ground forces or local authorities to take care of those little incidences of looting and mob violence. They did their job and he did his.

So where were the fucking cops? They should have been there by now. You'd think a 9-1-1 call about a shootout would have brought Sheriff Clemons charging up the Loop, guns blazing. He had the reputation. A real hotheaded son of a bitch. Yet Tallwood kept electing him because he supposedly didn't take any shit.

Manny didn't have much room to criticize since he refused to vote. Voting meant registering and registering put his name on another list in some bureaucratic office. No sir. He was on enough lists already. He didn't like lists.

Should have gone off the grid, he thought. *Moved away from people entirely*. Then he wouldn't be dealing with meth-head dealers living next door and getting their asses shot up during what otherwise was a beautiful night.

Someday soon. Once he'd saved enough. Then he'd be gone. Somewhere in the higher elevations. Away from—

BOOM. A shotgun blast.

Across the valley, familiar red and blue lights rotated on

top of Sheriff's vehicles.

About time, he thought.

A hellacious scream cut the valley in two. A roar of triumph followed. Beast one, man zero.

Seconds stretched. The Sheriff's vehicles stopped moving. Deputies shouted. Overlapping. The echo effect of the valley made it impossible to discern one from the other. It didn't matter as more shotguns opened fire.

What in the Hell is going on? Manny thought as he jumped to his feet. He raised the rifle and peered through the scope at the other side of the Loop, hoping to see something.

Too many damn trees and not enough moonlight.

Silence. No gunshots. No roars. The lights still rotated on the cruisers but that was it. Maybe they were all dead.

Feet scurried. No, raced. Snapping branches and stirring brush. Someone was running. Fleeing.

Another set of feet chased. Heavy. Thudding. Snapping rotten logs instead of sticks by the way it sounded. Manny glanced at the tops of the pines in the direction of the footfalls. Every few seconds one of the tops shifted against the wind.

It's chasing someone, he thought.

Whatever the thing was, it was down in the valley now. If that was the case, the cops hadn't stopped it. Which meant they were either dead or too chickenshit to pursue.

Shit. There was at least one camper down there. He'd ran into her at the 7-Eleven earlier. A woman in her mid-thirties buying beer. He'd overheard her asking the clerk how to reach the site.

Damn it, Manny thought. With the thing down there and innocent people down there, he didn't have much of a choice anymore. The Marine in him stopped resisting all together.

He turned and hustled down the steps of the deck and into the valley, rifle at the ready.

GABE

"Sheriff," Pronger said. "Maybe we shouldn't go up there."

Gabe bit his tongue, wondering the same thing. It wasn't a bear. He was dead sure about that. But whatever it was sounded like it was on a rampage and he didn't want to deal with an animal on a rampage in the dark.

More roars. Stanger jumped in the seat next to him. Gabe checked the side view. Lyle was staring up the drive, white as a sheet. He shifted to his other deputies. Pronger and Betts also gazed at the driveway, eyes glassy and wide, mouths hanging open.

Either get up there or get out of here, Gabe thought.

A shotgun blast reverberated down the driveway. Gabe's head jerked left, focusing on the gravel path. Some animal and some asshole with a gun. Meth involved. What the fuck was going on?

"Hit the lights," Gabe said.

"What?" Stanger said.

"You heard me. Time to go see what in Christ's name is happening up there."

Stanger reached for the switch. His fingers trembled. But he managed to flip the switch.

The rotating red and blues seemed to wake Pronger and Betts from their frightened dazes. They blinked and straightened up in their seats. Lyle, too, looked more alert. His eyes narrowing and lips tightening.

Gabe stuck his hand out the window and rotated it in a vertical circle several times. Then he pointed up the driveway. *High-ho Silver, away.*

Stanger shifted and accelerated, turning up the drive. Lyle followed. Pronger and Betts brought up the rear.

"Don't drive too fast," Gabe said. "We don't want some

crazy animal or asshole with a shotgun to run out in front of us."

Stanger eased off some on the gas. "Yeah, I don't want to run over a bear."

The roars were almost deafening as they reached the top of the drive. Gabe scanned the area but couldn't see anything. Stanger parked and Gabe grabbed a shotgun and got out.

The roars stopped. The other vehicles pulled up. Doors opened and closed behind Gabe. He turned and found all his deputies armed up and looking at the front door of the house.

"Busted open," Lyle said.

Stanger pumped his shotgun. Betts and Pronger followed suit.

"Betts, Pronger, take the front," Gabe said. "Lyle, take—"

The roar again. Gabe flinched as it echoed around him. Out of the corner of his eyes he saw some one run from behind the house into the woods.

"Shit, go, go." He took off running toward the back of the house, Stanger pounding behind him.

Something big and hairy bounded from behind the house. Gabe froze and Stanger ran into his back. The thing spun toward them, no more than ten feet away.

"Jesus." Gabe fired a round blindly and back peddled.

The buckshot hit but he didn't see where. The beast bellowed and closed toward them. Gabe grabbed Stanger and threw in front of him and retreated toward the car.

Stanger fired a round of his own as the thing reached for him. It hit him square in the chest and the bellow became a cry of anguish. But it didn't stop coming toward them.

Gabe studied its face for a second. Apelike. Sort of. Thick brown fur. Maniac eyes. Huge body.

Betts and Pronger stepped forward and fired. Stanger re-engaged. Gabe hung back and watched.

The next couple of shots tore hair and flesh from its right arm and part of its leg. It stopped advancing and turned and sprinted into the woods, breathing heavy and clutching its chest.

"Let's go get it," Pronger said.

"Hell yeah," Betts started to run toward the tree line.

"Hold fast," Gabe said.

"Come on, Sheriff, it's hurt pretty bad," Betts said.

"I said hold fast."

Betts kicked gravel. "Damn."

"Stop whining and secure the house. Pronger, go with him." Gabe turned and found Stanger staring where the beast had been. "You okay?"

Stanger blinked. His lips moved but it took a few seconds to form words. "I think so."

"Good." Gabe looked around for Lyle. Nowhere to be found. "Lyle? Where the hell are you?"

A hand shot up from behind the back end of one of the cars. "Over here, Sheriff."

Gabe grimaced. "It's gone. You can get up now."

Lyle rose. His whole body shook. "I was just taking cover to reload."

"Is that a fact." Gabe walked over to him and grabbed the barrel of the shotgun. "Pretty cold for having fired so many rounds."

Lyle swallowed and shrugged.

"Go secure the back of the house."

"But Sheriff—"

"Go secure the back of the house or I'll make you go into the woods after it."

Lyle swallowed again and glanced at the woods where the thing had disappeared. He nodded and walked toward the back of the house.

"Chicken shit," Stanger muttered.

"Let it be," Gabe said and moved over to the tree line. "How many rounds did it take?"

"A lot. Double ought buck, too."

"Got to be hurt pretty bad."

"You want to go after it?"

Gabe shook his head and turned to his deputy. "If there's one thing I learned watching scary movies, it's you don't go into the woods after a monster in the dark."

"Monster? Looked more like a gorilla."

"You ever seen a ten foot tall gorilla before?"

"Why I've never seen any gorilla before."

"I'll tell you then, they don't get to be ten feet tall."

"It wasn't a bear, Sheriff. That I'm sure of."

"Yeah it wasn't a bear."

"Then what the hell was it?"

"Well, if I had to hazard a guess, I'd say we just had an honest to God encounter with Bigfoot."

"There's no such thing as Bigfoot."

"Seeing is believing and I saw Bigfoot take a bunch of rounds of double ought buck before running away into these woods here."

Stanger lowered his shotgun and put his free hand on his hip and spat. "So this didn't involve drugs?"

"I'm not sure yet." Gabe motioned Stanger to follow. "Let's go around back and see what's what."

Around back, Lyle bent over and puked his dinner into a dead rose bush. Several feet away from him was a body with no arms, said arms nearby, and someone blown to hell by scattershot. A bunch of splintered wood, too. Busted chain.

"Holy shit." Stanger walked around the bodies, whistling. "This boy got his arms torn off right at the shoulder."

Gabe studied the scene. Guy with no arms had a shotgun on the ground near the corpse. Lot of damn shotguns out tonight. Other dude killed by a shotgun blast. Easy to put two and two together there.

He turned to the entrance down to the cellar. Busted hinges. Scrapped wood. Giant chains to the side. Huge locks.

On the ground near the entrance, a plastic bowl. Gabe squatted and picked it up. Covered with saliva. Little bit of white clear residue. He picked up a small chunk of glass.

Nope, not a piece of glass. Meth.

He set the bowl down and dropped the piece of meth in it. Then rose and walked to the edge of the cellar entrance. The distinct smell of shit and piss rose to greet him from within. Not regular shit. More like cow shit. Only stronger. Gabe thought about it for a moment. Sicker. Like a sick cow with the runs.

"Sheriff, this is Mickey Gannon," Stanger said. "He's covered in blood but it's him all right. I'd recognize his asshole face even if he didn't have one."

"That makes a lot of sense." Gabe kept his focus down the stairs, trying to make out as much of the cellar as possible. Shit puddles coated the floor. Some had merged with others to form a lake. Black footprints everywhere. Big footprints. Plastic bowls like the one he just held a second ago. He wagered they'd find meth residue in them as well.

"You think that guy we saw run into the woods was Russell?"

Gabe stepped away from the cellar, taking in the busted chains and door. "That would be a reasonable guess."

Footsteps. Gabe turned, shotgun at his hip. Betts and Pronger jogged around the side. When they saw what was left of Mickey, they skidded and stopped.

"Whoa." In unison.

"Inside secure?" Gabe said.

Betts nodded. "Two dead upstairs." He turned and pointed up at a busted window. "One tried to fly away."

Pronger had moved to the back of the lot and stood on top of a berm, shining his flashlight down the hillside. "Didn't fly too far."

"You see him?" Betts said.

"What's left of him." Pronger turned the light off and headed over to them. "Looks like he tried to kiss the inside of a tree trunk at high speed."

"This is one big mess," Stanger said.

"Don't go stating the obvious." Gabe turned to Lyle. "You okay?"

Lyle wiped his mouth the back of his hand. "I think so."

Stanger sidled up next to Gabe. "So what do you think was going on?"

"I think our boys Mickey and Russell stumbled into some shit they didn't expect."

"You mean Bigfoot?"

"What else would I mean?"

Stanger shrugged. "Just making sure."

"They came to eliminate their competition and ended up dealing with a fiending Sasquatch."

"Fiending? You think Bigfoot was going through withdrawal or something."

"That's exactly what I think."

Stanger laughed. Gabe didn't. Betts and Pronger walked over and they all formed a circle.

"Excuse me," Betts said. "But did you say we've got a hooked Bigfoot on our hands?"

"That's right."

Pronger scratched his head. "How in the hell did they get Bigfoot hooked?"

"It doesn't really matter how. We'll probably never know. Point is, our boys had themselves a Bigfoot trapped in their cellar and they were feeding it steady doses of meth."

"That's not good."

"No it isn't. Especially for Russell and anyone else who has the unfortunate luck to cross its path right now."

"Well we need to find it and kill it then," Stanger said. "We can't let that thing runaround in a withdrawal craze."

"No we can't." Gabe spat. "But we're not going after it."

"What?"

Gabe ignored Stanger and turned to Betts and Pronger. "Was there meth in the house?"

"Yes, Sheriff," Betts said. "Whole shit ton in the garage."

"Go get it. Bring on out here."

Betts and Pronger headed back into the house without another word.

"What are you planning?" Stanger said.

"Is that armored car still in the impound lot?"

"Yeah. Still smells like piss and shit, too."

Gabe smiled. A disgruntled worker who'd been laid off over the phone while doing a transport had decided to leave a couple of presents in the cab for his supervisor and walked off with the money. Parked it in a tow-away zone for good measure. It was scheduled for pick-up by the company next week. No doubt they'd be picking up a more heavily damaged vehicle than planned. But hey, this was police business. Serving the public good and all. Gabe figured they'd understand. And if they didn't? Fuck 'em.

"Take Lyle and go pick it up and bring it back here," Gabe said.

"Sheriff, are you going to clue me in on what we're doing?"

"We're going to catch it." Betts and Pronger came around the corner carrying clear plastic boxes of meth. "And here comes the bait."

RUSSELL

Branches whipped his face. His toes connected with a rock or log, sending him somersaulting head over heels. But he didn't stop. Didn't stay down. Russell jumped back up and kept sprinting. Because the giant feet still pounded behind him. They rumbled the earth with every fall. It sniffed the air, tracking his movements. He swore he could feel its breath on the back of his neck.

Keep running, Russell thought. *Stay ahead or end up like Mickey.*

Hell no. He'd kill himself first.

But he'd left the shotgun behind. Shit. All he had was the bag of money, bouncing and digging into his spine.

The footfalls grew louder. His stomach quaked under their drops. It growled. Not roared. No, it wanted him to know it was close. That it would have him soon.

Keep. Running.

Russell's thighs were on fire. The burn spread up his hips into his guts. He wanted to stop and throw up. He wanted quit. The adrenaline kept him going, though. It pumped what little energy he had through his limbs. It sharpened his vision, his hearing, helping compensate for the scattered moonlight peeking through the treetops.

Whoa!

Tree trunk. Russell slammed on the brakes, pivoted about forty degrees, and managed to make it around. His deltoid caught some bark and he felt it scrape skin through his shirt but there was no pain. Not yet at least.

There it was. A sharp needle-like stabbing throb spread into his shoulder. He felt something warm and wet trickling down his arm. Blood.

KEEP. RUNNING.

Flickering. Something flickering in the corner of his left eye. Russell risked a glance without slowing down. A fire. Campfire.

Something else. A shadow by the fire.

Oh, shit, he thought. *It's a person.*

KEEP. RUNNING.

He risked another glance. Sure enough, a woman. By herself, as far as he could tell.

KEEP! RUNNING!

If it was a dude, maybe he could. Just ignore him. Maybe pretend he never saw him. A woman though...

Russell slowed and altered course, heading for the fire. "Hey, lady!"

The woman leaned forward over the arm of her camping chair, squinting into the dark beyond the flames. She had a bottle of beer in her hand.

"Who's there?"

Russell was about twenty feet away. "You need to get up and run!"

"What?"

Ten feet. "Run!"

She jumped to her feet but remained still. She wore a 49ers jacket and blue jeans. Her dark hair was pulled back in a pony tail. "Who the hell are you? One of those assholes blasting *Seinfeld* and cop shows at the top of the hill?"

Russell skidded to a halt a few feet away from her. He bent over and grasped his knees, sucking air and coughing. "Cop shows?" he managed between breaths.

"Yeah, I heard gun shots."

"We need to go."

"Why?" Wood snapped in the dark. "What was that?"

"The reason we need to run."

Another snap. Sniffing.

"What is it?"

"No time now. It's close." A low growl. "It'll kill us."

Her eyes showed fear. She backed away from Russell as if he were the beast. "I-I-I—"

Fuck it, Russell thought. He reached out and grabbed her

arm. "We need to go. Now!"

"I-I—"

In the dark beyond the flames, Bigfoot roared. The woman screamed. Russell tensed up for a moment but his reflexes kicked in. He dragged the woman away as the beast bounded into the light.

"Oh my God!"

She moved with him. Russell stayed ahead of her, holding onto her hand as they sprinted deeper into the woods. Bigfoot roared again behind them. Its feet pounded earth, resuming the chase.

"What does it want?" she said.

"To kill us."

"Where are we going?"

"I don't know. Away from it."

They rounded a pine and scurried down a hollow. The woman tripped on something and went flying forward on her chest. Russell tried to catch her but lost his grip on her hand. She connected with something hard, crying out in pain. He bent over to help her up but she wasn't moving fast. She was barely moving at all.

"Come on, we got to move," Russell said, yanking up on her arm.

"I'm dizzy."

Russell noticed blood on her forehead. In the moonlight, it looked black. "Can you move?"

She took a step and lost her balance. Russell caught her this time.

Shit, he thought. Behind them, the thundering footfalls stopped. A few seconds of tense silence. Russell held his breath. He felt the woman at his side doing the same.

Something hit something in the darkness. Like a baseball slung into the side of a house.

"Did you hear that?" she said.

"Yeah."

Another moment passed.

Then the sniffing started. A roar followed.

"Fuck." Couldn't run. Not with her like this. He couldn't

leave her behind, either. Not now. Not after basically leading the thing to her.

The footfalls resumed. It was close.

There, he thought. He pulled the woman over to a tree. There was a boulder near the trunk. Above it a limb. Maybe they could climb it.

"What are we doing?" she said, wiping blood from her eyes with her sleeve.

"Get up on that rock."

She didn't ask anything more. She managed to pull herself up. Russell followed. He almost slipped but righted himself before sliding face first back down. They were a good four feet above the forest floor now.

"Come here," Russell said. "I'm going to boost you up."

Again, the woman didn't say anything. She let Russell wrap his arms around her hips and lift.

"Can you reach it?"

"Yeah."

Russell couldn't see but felt her weight diminish in his grasp as she pulled herself up. Behind him, the footfalls grew louder. They seemed like they were on top of him.

He turned on the top of the boulder in time to see Bigfoot sprint from behind a tree toward him. Russell's eyes widened and he jumped and caught hold of the limb.

"Hurry," she said.

Splinters bit into his hands as he pulled up. He managed to get his right elbow over the branch. Below, Bigfoot roared and jumped on the boulder. It pawed at his dangling feet. Russell flailed his legs and connected with its head. It bought him enough time to swing his left foot onto the limb. His right still drifted in space.

Bigfoot didn't go for his stray foot, though. Instead, he felt its fingers trying to grab the bag on his back. Its putrid breath baked his neck. If it got a hold of the bag, it could rip him and the whole branch down.

Russell swung his other foot onto the branch and pulled himself the rest of the way up. He looked around for the woman.

"Up here."

He looked up. She was already another three branches above him.

He hurried, managing to get to his feet while moving his hands to the trunk for balance. Bigfoot roared again and jumped and grabbed the branch. The whole tree shuddered under its weight.

Beneath his feet, the wood creaked and then cracked like a thunderclap. Russell leapt for the next branch above as the other snapped free from the trunk. He grimaced as he scratched and clawed to hang on.

It took a minute or so to regain a firm hold. Once he had it, Russell pulled up and sat on the branch just below the woman. His arms and shoulders burned as much as his thighs. His lungs fought hard for air. Dizziness squeezed his head.

"You think it's dead?"

Russell rubbed his temples. "What?"

"Look."

He blinked and glanced down at the ground. Bigfoot lay on its back to the side of the boulder. "Fell when the branch broke?"

"Hit the rock on the way down. Sounded like it snapped its back."

Could we be that lucky? Russell thought. He squinted, trying to improve his vision. It took a few moments to adjust but his night vision sharpened enough to make out the beast's chest rising and falling in shallow waves.

"It's still breathing."

She sighed. "Maybe we can get down and head for the Loop."

"You want to risk your neck that it won't wake up as soon as you hit the ground?" She didn't answer. "Me neither."

"What happens when it wakes up?"

"It'll probably go bat shit crazy and try to get us again." *Because it's a junkie and hasn't made it through the withdrawals yet.* "Hopefully it'll go away once it realizes it can't reach us."

"Or it'll just knock the whole damn tree down."

Russell leaned back against the trunk and wondered if the

thing could actually knock something this big down. Then he remembered what it did to Mickey. If it could rip someone apart so easily in a drug-fiend craze, what was a tree to it once the withdrawal got worse? No, they needed to start thinking of another way to get out of this mess. Waiting up here wasn't the answer.

He wished he had his pipe. A hit would help. It'd clear the cob webs. Help him think straight. Definitely would ease the fire raging in his muscles and joints.

"You're bleeding," she said and pointed at his shoulder where a section of his shirt had been torn away.

Russell checked it out. Nice little gash but nothing too bad. He motioned at her forehead. "You, too."

She wiped more out of her eyes and pulled a tissue from her jacket pocket and pushed it against the wound. "What's your name, by the way?"

"Huh?"

"Your name, what is it?"

"Russell. Yours?"

"Persephone. Everyone calls me Seph, though."

"Okay." He cleared his throat. "I wish I could say it's nice to meet you."

Seph chuckled. "Yeah, me too. Pretty hard to believe."

"That's one way of putting it."

Russell chewed on his bottom lip and tried to figure out what to do next. They couldn't stay up in the tree much longer. But he had no idea what to do next.

"I think we need to find a way—"

Russell broke off when he heard movement. He looked down to find Bigfoot rolling onto its side.

MANNY

It hadn't been hard to track and locate. The continuous pounding of the earth. The labored breathing followed by frenzied sniffing. The snapping of limbs and bouncing off of tree trunks. Anyone could have found it. When Manny did, he couldn't believe his eyes.

It's Bigfoot, he thought when he first saw it through the scope. The moonlight illuminated the crazed eyes and savage maw of the beast. He couldn't make out much more than that. There was little doubt what it was. The facial features, prominent brow, and an almost cone-like skull were all too familiar from the thousands of artist renderings seen on television specials and tabloid journal reports. **Woman Escapes Bigfoot in Northern California** with a pencil sketch of the monster under the headline. Or one of those *Monster Hunter*-type shows on Discovery or History Channel with all its fancy computer animation. There were differences here and there. More hair, less hair, bigger teeth. But essentially the same across the media.

Manny hated to admit it but they'd been pretty much dead on with their renderings. Which meant there had been some truth to those loonies and their encounters. At least a few of them.

Now I'm one of the loonies, he thought.

He remained downwind of the creature, staying about three hundred feet away. He kept it in the crosshairs when he could. He didn't plan on shooting it but if it caught on to him and decided to charge, he didn't want to be surprised. If he had to fire, he wasn't sure the bullet would have an impact. Not a center mass shot, at least. He glimpsed several wounds across the creature's torso as it sprinted in and out of the moonlight. Looked like the deputies had tried to stop it with scattershot before it made it into the woods.

Then he saw what it was after. Some skinny guy ran for his life. Bigfoot wasn't running away from people, it was pursuing. A predator after its prey.

What the hell did that poor son of a bitch do to end up in this fix? Then Manny remembered his own position and realized he could end up much the same way if he wasn't careful.

Manny pursued at a brisk pace for several hundred feet before stopping and finding the creature again in the scope. It had changed course several times, keeping pace with the guy who was trying like hell to shake the beast. Manny did the best he could to maintain his distance but the thing was fast. Determined. Still in pursuit. The skinny guy broke off suddenly on a perpendicular course. Toward flickering light.

A campfire, Manny thought. *Shit.*

The guy screamed, "Run!"

Shit, shit, shit.

Manny sprinted forward to another tree, took up shelter behind it and re-scoped. He saw a woman standing by the fire talking to the guy. The guy was animated but Manny couldn't hear him or the woman.

Where the hell was the creature?

There. In the darkness outside the firelight. Watching.

The fire seemed to keep it at bay. But for how long?

He lined up the shot, centering the crosshairs on the massive skull. Deep breath. Hold it.

It roared. The guy and girl took off running. It followed. Fast. Too fast for Manny to get the shot.

Son of a bitch!

He pursued. Sprinting. He needed to close the gap to get another shot.

His lungs burned. It'd been a long time since he'd expended this kind of energy. Big time out of shape.

Manny stopped again and raised the rifle and peered down the scope. He found the guy and girl, standing in a hollow. Listening. Quiet. Blood on her forehead. No Bigfoot. Where the hell—

It roared to his left. Manny dropped to a knee and swung the rifle in the direction of the bellow, ready to fire as soon as he acquired the contact. Before he could, though, something hard and dense struck his cheek and jaw. He rocked and fell on his back. Green spots and a strange blackness floated in his field of vision. Pine trees stretched up toward heaven. He heard screams and thunder crack. Then all of it faded.
Faded.
Faded.

GABE

"Sheriff, we've got a problem."

Gabe winced and cued the radio. "What is it?"

"Battery's dead on this armored truck," Stanger said. "This fucker ain't going anywhere."

Shit, Gabe thought. "Did you try jumping it?"

"Yeah. No-go."

Well fuck me. "All right, get back up here pronto."

"You don't want me to try and find a replacement?"

"Don't have that kind of time. We'll just have to improvise."

"How so?"

"Get back up here. I'm not going to discuss it on the radio."

"On our way."

Gabe clenched the radio and almost threw it into the side of the cabin. "Mother fucker!"

"Problem, Sheriff?" Pronger said.

Yeah, big fucking problem. Now what? Got a bunch of meth and a raging meth-hooked Bigfoot and nothing to trap the son of a bitch in. Can't even secure it in the cellar since it destroyed the fucking door.

Slow down and think. "Don't worry about it, Pronger."

"What do you want me to do with this meth?"

Stick it up your ass. "Just set it down. Take a break and be back here with Betts in five minutes."

"I'm going to go inside and take a quick leak."

"I don't fucking care. What I do care about is you and Betts being back here in five minutes. Got it?"

Pronger nodded and ambled toward the front of the cabin. Gabe watched him the whole way. Then he looked down at the meth. How long had it been since he'd had a taste? Three years? Maybe four?

Fuck it, he thought.

He squatted in front of one of the bins, grabbed a baggie, and dumped a few rocks into his hand. He unclipped his Leatherman from his belt, unfolded the pliers, and started crushing the rocks. It took a few seconds. Once done, he snorted pinch after pinch until the handful was gone.

Hot damn! he thought and jumped to his feet. He hopped up and down for a minute, bobbing his head back and forth like a prize fighter. Oh that felt good. Energy coursed down his arms to the tips of his fingers. Euphoric and orgasmic all in one.

Gabe slipped the remainder of the baggie in his pocket and paced back and forth. Back and forth. Thinking. Brain storming. Planning. Yeah, planning. He had it figured out. All at once. Like a fucking waterfall of knowledge. Crystal clear. He couldn't believe he hadn't thought of it before. Armored truck? Stupid, stupid, stupid. He didn't want this thing alive. Dead, dead, deadskie. Had to be. Only way to ensure control. Plus, he was still going to bag a ton of dough with the body of Bigfoot. Real proof one of those motherfuckers exist? Fucking priceless!

"Sheriff."

Gabe stopped pacing, turned, and found Betts and Pronger staring at him. "What?"

"You were talking out loud about proof and dough and Bigfoot."

I was? Shit, need to simmer down and maintain. "I said be back here in five minutes."

"It's been five minutes," Betts said.

Gabe checked his watch. Damn, time flies when you're fucking high. "Okay, we need to get to work."

"Should we wait for Stanger and Lyle?" Pronger said.

"No, we've already wasted too much time." Gabe scratched the side of his neck. "Besides, we need them here for the climax. Before that, we need to lay the groundwork."

"What do you want us to do?"

Gabe pointed at one of the bins. "Grab a bunch of baggies and go down into the woods. I don't know, about a half mile. Start sprinkling the rocks every few feet all the way back here."

Pronger and Betts looked at the tree line before turning

back to Gabe. Their eyes were wide and faces slack.

"You want us to go into the woods?" Betts said.

"That's what I fucking said, wasn't it?"

"Yeah, but Bigfoot's in there."

"That's right. So we need to lure him back here."

"By making a trail of meth," Pronger said.

"Ding-ding we have a fucking winner." Gabe cackled and stomped his foot. "Now grab them baggies and get to fucking work."

"Sheriff, I don't know if this is a good idea," Betts said.

Gabe pulled his .38 and scratched his cheek with the barrel. "Betts, you wouldn't know a good idea if it shot you in the fucking eye, would you?"

Betts winced as if already shot. He followed the gun as Gabe lowered it back to his side. "No, I wouldn't I guess."

"That's right. Since I'm *the* Sheriff and you're *my* deputy, grab some baggies and head on into those woods. Don't like it, quit and run for Sheriff."

"Sheriff," Pronger said. "It's just, well, we don't know where that thing is down there."

"Based on all the roaring and howling, I'd say on the other side of the fucking valley. If you two—" Gabe pointed at Pronger and then Betts with the gun. "—don't want to have a run in with it, I'd recommend you get the meth planted right quick. Now go on."

Pronger and Betts moved to the bin and started stuffing baggies in every empty pocket they had. Gabe stood over them, motioning them to hurry up by waving the gun in circular motions. He tapped his foot and shook his head.

"Faster, people."

"That's all the room we've got," Betts said.

"What about inside your shirts? Stuff it like you're stealing food from the shelter."

Pronger and Betts opened their shirts and stuffed away. By the time they were done, they looked like they'd each gained about twenty pounds.

"Good," Gabe said. "Now off into the woods you go, fat boys."

Betts moved to the tree line. Pronger eyed Gabe who shooed him with the gun. He joined Betts and both looked over their shoulders one last time at their Sheriff.

"Do you two want me to fire your asses? Because I fucking will. Trust me you don't want to test me on this. Actually, you don't ever want to test me. But on this one, you don't even want to consider testing me. Got that?"

Both turned back around and took their first steps into the woods. A few seconds later, Gabe couldn't see them at all. Like the trees swallowed them whole.

The imagery made him laugh. Then he thought of that whore Tawny swallowing his cock. Yeah, that had felt good. Real good. Could go for some more of that actually.

Too bad there wasn't any snatch around. Well, there were some other cabins on the Loop. There had to be a single gal in one of them.

No, didn't have time for that. Just going to have to wait. Wait, wait, wait. Sure would be nice to get off before having the showdown with Bigfoot, though.

Who says you can't? he thought.

Gabe looked around, making sure Stanger and Lyle weren't back yet. Then he walked over to the side of the house and slid behind a bush and whipped out his already erect dick and started jacking away.

RUSSELL

"Now what are we going to do?" Seph said in a panicked whisper.

"Shhh!" Russell watched Bigfoot stumble to the side and almost fall before regaining his feet by hugging another tree trunk.

"We can't stay—"

"Maybe he'll forget we're up here." His voice was a calm whisper. "He took a hard fall. Just chill."

Bigfoot's shoulder rose and fell on heavy breaths. It pushed away from the tree but kept its right hand on it for balance. It didn't look up.

Russell licked his lips and thought, *Just go, dude. I don't have any glass. Go back to the cabin and load up on whatever's left. I'm sure the cops beat feet in terror thinking you might come back.*

Sniffing. It started sniffing.

Ah, hell.

Bigfoot's head slowly started to cant upward, tracing the trunk it used as a cane. Once it realize nothing was above it, it started to search other trees. Sniffing and sniffing. It went from one to another to another. A circle.

Seph tensed at his side and would have uttered a panicked squeak had he not put a hand on her thigh and pushed his left index finger against his lips. Shhh. She nodded.

Another tree. Another tree. Bigfoot came full circle almost. It past the boulder and started to move back to where it started. How it didn't see them, Russell wasn't sure. Probably had double vision from the fall. Or maybe it couldn't see that high now. The moon had fallen behind a small cloud. Slightly darker than it had been earlier.

It stopped. It was on the other side of the boulder, still

looking up. Sniffing. Russell held his breath. He wondered if it could hear his heart going THUD, THUD.

No movement. Just standing there, looking up. Sniffing. Sniffing.

Russell looked it in the eyes. *How can it not see me?* He felt sweat on his lips. Tasted salt as some ran into the corners of his mouth.

The cloud moved off into the night. As it did, the moonlight grew brighter in its wake. It wiped away the darkness that had hidden them. Bigfoot's eyes grew wider. Its nostrils flared.

"Oh, shit," Seph said.

Bigfoot roared. It reared back and hammered the trunk with both fists. Russell's nails dug into bark as he latched on to the tree.

Pound, pound, roar, pound. Over and over. Seph screamed at his side. He looked over and saw she had both arms wrapped around her branch, completely horizontal on it.

"What did you do to piss it off?" she said between belts of fear.

"I didn't do shit."

"It was chasing you."

Pound, pound, roar, pound. Pine needles and smaller branches began to hit his head from above.

"Yeah, it was chasing me. But I didn't do shit to it."

"It's bleeding."

"That's because the Sheriff's bitches shot it."

"Why'd it chase you?"

"I don't fucking know."

Pound, pound, roar, pound.

Another scream as the tree rocked violently to the left. Seph locked both legs around the branch in a death squeeze. Russell felt like he was trying to outlast a mechanical bull set on high.

"Why is it so mad?"

It didn't sound like she was asking him but God. Russell bit his tongue on another violent jerk. He spat blood and cursed and said, "Cuz he's a fucking strung out meth head."

"What?"

Pound, pound, roar, pound.

"It's hooked on meth."

"How do you—"

Holy shit, Russell thought and stopped listening to Seph and the beast flipping out below. He grabbed the bag off his back and opened it and started digging through the cash. Another violent jerk almost sent it from his hands but he managed to hang on to the shoulder strap. Next to him, he heard Seph's branch crack.

She screamed, louder than anything previous, as the branch fell. But it didn't break all the way. It snapped halfway through. She dangled at a forty-five.

Russell breathed a quick bit of relief and dug faster.

"Give me your hand," she said.

"I can't." Fingers between rolls of twenties.

"What?"

"I can't."

"I'm going to fall, you son of a bitch. Help me."

It's got to be in here, he thought. "I just need a second."

"For what?"

Pound, pound, roar, pound. The tree buckled. The branch fell even more. Seph hung at a seventy now.

"For the love of God, help me."

There, Russell thought. His fingers closed around a baggie. He yanked it out. Glass.

He tossed it down, watching it sway back and forth like a leaf falling to the ground. Bigfoot caught sight of it. It stopped pounding and roaring. It only watched as the little bag seemed to float down to it. Hands cupped, it raised them and caught it.

Then it tore it up and sniffed everything within in less than a second. It licked it fingers. It moaned.

Russell reached over and helped Seph over to his branch. As he did, she said, "What the hell was that about?"

"Crank. It wanted crank."

Seph looked down. "He's seriously hooked on meth?"

"Yeah."

"How do you know all this?" She looked at him. Eyes tight and full of anger. "How did meth end up in your bag?"

She looked the contents of the bag. "A bag full of money?"

"It's a long story."

"You're a drug dealer."

"No shit."

"So you got it hooked. Some kind of joke that went wrong."

"No, I didn't do shit to it."

"You led it to me. It was chasing you and your bag of meth. It wouldn't have done anything to me."

"I didn't know the meth was in the bag."

"So it's not your bag?"

"No—wait. Look, I said it's a long story."

"So you stole it."

Russell started to say more but stopped. What was the point? He didn't need this shit right now anyway. No, what he needed was to get out of this motherfucking tree.

He dug down into the bag, searching for more glass. If he could find another baggie or two, he could distract Bigfoot enough to climb down and head the other way. Seph could come if she wanted but he wasn't going to sit here and try to explain his life story anymore.

Below, Bigfoot released a long, tremendous sigh. It sounded like the climax of an orgasm. Then it looked back up. The eyes were still wild. Still full of fury. But sedated somewhat. No longer on the brink of starvation. Still hungry for more, sure, but not destroy-everything-in-its-path hungry.

"Is there more in there?" Seph said.

"I can't find anymore."

"Then why won't it leave?"

"How the fuck am I supposed to know?"

"You shot it didn't you? That's why it's bleeding from all over its chest."

Russell quit rummaging through the bag. "Look, I didn't shoot it. It just started chasing me. Obviously, now, because it could smell the meth in the bag."

"Who shot it then?"

"The fucking Sheriff and his deputies!"

Seph shook her head. "I knew it. You got caught stealing

drugs and somehow that poor creature got stuck in the middle."

"Poor creature? Lady, that fucking thing tore my partner's arms out of their sockets. Literally."

"What did you expect? People getting it hooked on meth. People shooting it. You think it asked for all this?"

"You think I did? Christ."

Below, Bigfoot kept its stare. It seemed like it was trying to decide what to do next. Keep watch or resume the assault on the tree. Russell had little doubt if Seph kept running her mouth, it would choose the latter.

"It's not going to leave," Seph said. "It's not going to leave and you don't have any more drugs and soon its high will wear off and then it'll knock this damn tree down and kill us all because of you and your druggie kind."

"Will you shut. The. Fuck. Up?" His fingers found two more baggies. He exhaled, relieved, at least for a few moments, and tossed them down. "You can be pissed at me all you want but let's try to make it through this first."

Seph grunted but refrained from saying anything else. Below, Bigfoot finished of the second baggie. His eyes dulled. Content. Yeah, Russell had seen that look before. Many times. In the mirror. Almost wished he'd kept a taste for himself.

No, man, he thought. *Keep your head straight. The last thing you need is another round of meth coursing through you.*

Bigfoot released the longest sigh Russell had ever heard. He watched the hairy beast shiver.

"What was that?" Seph said.

Russell shrugged in the darkness. A moment later, Bigfoot swayed a little and then stumbled off. It made it a few feet before it dropped straight down on its ass. Its head hung over its chest, chin way down. Its hands lay at its sides, palms up.

"I think it just hit the wall," Russell said.

"It's asleep?"

"Passed out describes it better. But yeah, out like a light."

"Can we get down?"

Russell kept a wary eye on the beast for a moment, wondering how deep into dreamland it had delved. And for how long?

Doesn't matter, he thought. *You need to get down now or risk not having another chance.*

"I think we need to try," Russell said. "Might be our only shot."

"What if it wakes up?" Again, that panicked tone. "What if it wakes up when we're on the ground and it—" Russell started climbing down. "Wait, what are you doing?"

"What's it look like? I don't know how long it'll be out but I want to be down and far away when it comes to."

Seph rose up enough to peer down over Russell's shoulder at Bigfoot. She licked her lips and nodded to herself. Convincing herself.

"Okay, okay. I'm coming, too."

Great, he thought.

It took a few minutes to climb down. The closer he got to the ground, the slower Russell moved, worried the tiniest sound might bring Bigfoot raging back into the world of consciousness. He half expected a piece of bark to fall or twig to snap. None did, thankfully. When he reached the surface, he held his breath and clenched his jaw, and placed one foot down on the pine needle carpet, followed by the other.

Across from him, Bigfoot's shoulder rose and fell on heavy breaths. It wheezed on the exhalations. It also smelled awful. A combination of drying blood, addicts musk, and soiled fur.

Seph gagged and covered her mouth next to him. He gave her a hard stare and pressed his index finger vertically against his lips. Her eyes watered but she nodded and kept from puking all over him.

The bag of money once again hung across his back. He motioned Seph to follow him and started taking one step backwards away from the beast. A second step. Then third, fourth and fifth. Slow all the way.

Bigfoot didn't shift. It maintained a constant ratio of labored inhalations to wheezy exhalations.

I guess ripping a guy's arms out and getting shot with a bunch of .00 buck really can take it out of you, Russell thought.

Once they were a couple of trees away, he risked turning his back to it and picked up the pace.

"Where are we going?" Seph said in a low but rushed whisper.

"Hell, I don't' know. Away from it for now. Figure we got time to stop and get pointed in the right direction once we're not worried about it waking up and tearing us in half."

"Maybe I'll just head in a different direction now. I think I know the way back to my site."

"Go for it. But remember, you're site isn't that far away from where we ended up."

"When I need advice from a meth dealer, I'll ask."

Russell slammed on the brakes and turned to her. She almost ran into him but managed to stop a few inches short.

"Look, I'm sorry I dragged you into this. I thought I was helping, all right. But if you say one more smart ass thing about me and drugs or blame me for this shit again I will knock the piss out of you."

Seph's lips tightened, as did her eyes. Almost daring him.

"By the way," Russell said, "I can smell the beer on you. Didn't see anyone else in your camp. My guess, you were staring at the fire and tying one on, right?"

"How dare you? You've got no idea."

A sense of victory spread through Russell. "You're damn right. And neither do you. Remember that next time before you go pointing that boney ass finger of blame at people."

"Fuck you," she said and turned and started to walk away.

Russell reached out for her arm but missed. "Wait a minute."

"No."

"Where are you going?"

"Doesn't matter. Away from you and it."

"Come back." Russell hurried to keep up. "It's not smart to be out here on your own."

Seph turned suddenly. He noticed her arm swinging toward him. He heard her knuckles connect with his jaw. And then he found himself sitting on his ass, pain creeping up his tailbone.

"Stay the fuck away from me." She stood over him, fist clenched. "I was fine before you showed up. I plan to be that way again."

Russell grimaced and rubbed his jaw and held up his other hand in surrender. "Fine. Go. Sorry I ever met you."

"Feeling's mutual."

Seph turned away and moved off into the woods. What direction, he had no idea. He wanted to say he didn't care either but couldn't. Yeah, she was annoying but if she ended up in that thing's clutches later...

Don't think about it, Russell thought. *It's her call. Now worry about yourself and get the hell out of here.*

Right.

Russell looked around him. First eye level and then up the trees toward the moon. Which way?

He didn't know. East, west. Hell, he barely knew up from down. All he did know was Bigfoot was behind him. So heading away from it was the first priority.

Move already then, he thought and climbed to his feet. Russell shifted and looked behind him for a moment, making sure the beast wasn't awake and stalking him. Nope. Nothing but trees. He couldn't even see the top of the thing's head from where he stood.

Time to get gone. Russell looked where Seph was before she disappeared out of sight. Then he stepped in the direction perpendicular to her path.

MANNY

He clenched Chris's hand, blood oozing between pressed flesh. He wanted to say it was going to be okay, wanted to tell his spotter, his friend, it was just a scratch. But the screams choked the words off before they could come.

Chris halted his wailing long enough to say, "Mister, are you okay?"

No, he hadn't said that.

"Mister, are you okay?"

It wasn't Chris's voice. Not even a man's voice. Definitely a woman. But there was Chris, on the ground, dying. Talking like a girl.

"Mister, you need to get up because there's a monster in the woods."

Monster? What?

The creature. Bigfoot. He'd been tracking it. Tracking until—

Manny fluttered his eyes only to be rocked by seething pain in his head. It stretched all the way down into his jaw. Even his teeth hurt. He reached up and touched where the rock had hit him. Matted hair and blood.

But you're alive, he managed to think. *Get up Marine*.

His vision shifted from blurred to somewhat out of focus. A woman knelt over him. Not young but not old. Not pretty but not ugly. Tired. She looked very tired.

"Mister, we need to move."

Manny coughed and eased himself into a sitting position. He still clenched the rifle. The woman had not been foolish enough to try and pry it from his grip. Good for her. Although unconscious he had no doubt the old reflexes would have kicked in. He also doubted he would have been able to control himself if they had. A key to a sniper's survival was his rifle.

No one got a hold of it. Ever.

He lifted it from the dirt and lowered it onto his lap and took in his surroundings with quick glances. Still dark. The moon hadn't moved much. Must have been out, what, twenty minutes.

"You saw it?" he said and winced from the pain in his jaw and ear. Then he realized he recognized her. The woman standing with the guy by the fire. Right before he got nailed with the rock.

"Saw it? It almost killed me."

"How did you get away?"

"Climbed up a tree."

"And it left? What direction?"

"It didn't exactly leave."

"What do you mean?"

She told the story of a meth dealer named Russell and a bag of money. Money and a few baggies of meth he managed to drop down to the enraged creature.

"You're saying Bigfoot is a meth addict?" Manny had a tough time swallowing it but, if true, it explained a lot about the cabin and what he thought was just *Animal Planet* blasting all the time.

"It's true."

"And it passed out?"

"Yes."

"How far away?"

"I'm not sure. I haven't been walking long. Maybe five minutes."

Manny nodded, calculating in his head. "It's in the direction opposite of where you're kneeling right now?"

"Yes. Can we go now?"

"The man who was with you, where is he now?"

"I give two shits about that guy."

"He was heading away from it, too, though, correct?"

"Yes, damn it."

Manny rose. His balance was shaky but he managed to keep his feet. He rested the rifle in the crook of his left arm and surveyed the wood around him one more time. Listening. No movement other than the trees swaying in the wind.

"And no one else was being pursued?"

"No. Russell said his partner was killed by it. That's all I know."

Good, Manny thought. It was injured from the shots it took from the Sheriff and his merry band of fuck-ups. It was slumbering in a meth dream world. Between the narcotic and loss of blood, maybe it would never wake up. And if it did wake up, it would start looking for another source of meth. After all, it was only chasing the one guy because of the meth stashed in the money. Manny didn't have to worry about innocent people getting hurt because it hadn't killed him, even though he was armed. It could have easily but it chose to disable him, not rip his arms out. If it happened to live and a few more meth pushers died as a result, what was the problem with that?

"Do you know of any other people camping down here in the valley?"

She shook her head. "Haven't seen any."

"Okay, then I say we head for my place. I have a cabin up on the Loop. We can shelter there until dawn. If nothing else happens, I'll take you to your car. Sound fair?"

"Why can't I go to my car now?"

"Your car is close to where that thing is currently passed out. Start-up that engine and you might wake it up."

"That's what Russell said."

"Sorry but he was right. Now I don't think it'll go after someone who doesn't have meth on them. But then again it's not exactly a predictable animal right now. So, we ere on the side of caution and wait a few hours."

She nibbled on her bottom lip for a moment before shrugging. "Fine. What's your name, by the way?"

"Manny. Yours?"

"Persephone but everyone calls me Seph."

"Nice to meet you. Follow me."

THE AMATEURS

Guy had to take a piss. Bad. He stirred in the sleeping bag and fluttered his eyes. His dick ached. He reached down and rubbed his rock hard pee boner, hoping to soothe some of the pain away. It didn't work.

He sighed and flipped the sleeping bag flap open and sat up. His head was light and the tent was dark, creating a feeling of floating in an abyss. Guy ran his hand along the side of the floor until his fingers hit the flashlight. He clicked it and portions of the darkness retreat under the beam.

Across from him, Bunny lay on her side, ass to him. Bare. He frowned when he noticed the dried semen streaks on both cheeks. Bitch couldn't even take the time to wipe it off while it was still wet.

Probably because she was more interested in getting high rather than cleaning up, Guy thought. *And that's while they'll always be amateurs.*

He shrugged it off. Amateurs, yes, but still bringing him in a nice bit of cash. Soon he'd have enough to hire some real talent. Then Bunny and Kitten would find themselves back on the streets, blowing junkies for meth.

Speaking of Kitten…

Guy swept the light to the opposite side. Kitten lay in the same position he'd last seen her in. Curled up, thumb in her mouth. Twenty-years-old and still a thumb sucker. She'd gotten so high earlier she couldn't keep the camera steady. Ended up passing out. Which pissed Guy off because he had to film the anal scene with Bunny himself. Not a bad P.O.V. but it was, for lack of a better word, a pain in the ass to fumble with the camera while trying to keep his dick in Bunny's backdoor.

"What are you doing?"

Guy swung the light back at Bunny, hitting her with the

full beam right in the eyes. She cringed and held up her hand and turned away.

"What the fuck, Guy?"

Guy laughed. "You need to wipe your ass."

"You need to get that fucking light out of my eyes."

Guy directed the light at the entrance of the tent. "How many times do I have to tell you to clean up after scenes? What if I wanted to film something right now? We'd have to scrape jizz of your ass for half an hour first."

"I was fucking tired, okay?"

Guy snorted. "You took a hit and followed Kitten there to dreamland."

"Is she still alive?"

"You think she's dead?"

"She hit the wall pretty hard. She's been smoking all day."

Guy hit Kitten with the light. "Still breathing."

"Doesn't look like it."

"See how her tits are moving. That means she's breathing. Besides, you can hear her sucking that thumb clear across the valley."

"Yeah, I guess you can."

Guy pushed up to his knees and grabbed the zipper to the entrance. "Be right back."

The flame from a lighter illuminated the tent. Bunny lit her pipe and inhaled and said, "Where are you going?" Smoke followed.

"To take a piss. Can't leave it alone, can you?" *Good thing I get it free from that meth head with the glasses on the Loop. Well, not for free. But not an unfair trade, either. Cheap amateur porn in exchange for hundreds of dollars of meth. Not fair at all.* Guy laughed on the inside.

"Just a small hit." Bunny inhaled again and coughed. "Why do you care?"

"I don't."

Guy unzipped the entrance and crawled out into the night. His Crocs were right there. He slipped them on and started to trudge toward the nearest tree when he heard rustling behind him. He turned and found Bunny crawling out behind him.

Her breasts pale in the moonlight, her nipples dark and firm.

She's not bad looking, Guy thought. Be nice if she put on some weight. Needed a boob job but her tits weren't bad as is. Just too damn skinny. If she were a little thicker, he might keep her on. Kitten, no way. Too much drama there. But Bunny had potential.

"Can I tag along?" Bunny said.

"You want to watch me pee?"

"No, I need to go, too."

"Find your own tree."

"I'm scared."

"To pee?"

"To pee alone."

Guy rubbed the ache in his dick again. "I don't have time for this bullshit."

He walked away. Bunny followed, saying, "I had a crazy nightmare."

"Was a vampire biting you while you peed?"

"No. But I heard some kind of monster roaring. Never saw it in the dream, just heard it. And then there were these cops shooting into the woods. But they couldn't see it either."

Guy reached a tree. He stood and tried to coax his hard-on down enough so he could piss more than a drop at a time. "Probably all the *Animal Planet* we've been hearing from the Loop. Crept into your dreams is all."

"And the guns?"

"Maybe they switched it to a cop show." Drop, drop but no stream yet.

Bunny squatted on the other side of the tree. The sound of piss hitting dirt soon followed. Guy hoped it would help stimulate his own release but nada. Just another drop followed by an ache all the way up the shaft. Needed to get rid of the hard-on.

Bunny came around the tree trunk. "Finished?"

Guy closed his eyes and gritted his teeth. "No."

"What's the problem?"

"Problem is you're breaking my concentration."

"To pee?"

"I have a pee hard-on."

"Those are real? I figured you were just turned on from a dream or something."

"No, they're real and sometimes they hurt when you have to pee."

"So what are you going to do?"

Guy grabbed her by the arm and pulled her over and turned her around so she faced the tree. "Get rid of the hard-on." He spit on his hands and rub it up and down his shaft.

"I'm pretty dry right now."

Guy spit on his hand again and pushed his palm between her legs and rubbed her labia. Bunny arched her back and moaned. Guy squatted slightly and spread her lips with the same hand while pushed the head of his dick in with the other.

She was dry but that only lasted a few seconds. If Bunny was good at one thing, it was getting wet. Guy pumped away.

Bunny braced her hands against the tree trunk and pushed back into Guy. Soon, the sensation of needing to pee gave way to the pleasure receptors firing on all cylinders. It was moments like this that Guy liked the most. Doing whatever he wanted for whatever reason he wanted with his girls.

"Do you ever feel like there's not much to life?" Bunny said.

Guy pumped faster, ignoring her. Why did she do this? Earlier, during the anal scene, she kept asking what he thought of the drug violence on the border. She didn't seem to understand that viewers wanted to hear her moan and scream "Fuck me harder!" not her opinion on cross-border crime.

"Like this is it. This is all there is." She braced and shot her ass back into him harder than ever, just as he plunged into her to the hilt. Guy moaned. "Like all we're meant to be is filler while the important people get the bigger parts in the movie that's life."

Guy death-gripped her hips and hammered as hard as he could and said, "Will you shut the fuck up?"

She did, deciding to try and meet him slam for slam. After a few more seconds, Guy pulled out. Bunny, well trained, turned around and dropped to her knees in time to get the full blast on her face. Guy sighed as a few more hot globs hit her neck and breasts.

He backed away and looked down. Bunny was wiping goo from her left eye and cheek. Then she licked it off her fingers. Good girl.

Bunny looked up at him. "I mean it's just sad that this may be all there is. We're here to make these movies and make some money but that's it. Small parts to play. Parts no one will ever really give a shit about."

Guy rubbed his forehead and moved to the other side of the tree to finally take that piss. "Yeah, sucks being filler."

"Sometimes I think I should have stayed in school."

Guy pinched of the piss before the first drop came out. "Bunny, go back to the tent and grab the camera."

"Why?"

"Well, we haven't done a golden shower scene yet. Seems like the perfect opportunity. I got the piss ready to go."

Bunny rose and started toward the tent. "And now I'm going to get peed on. Talk about useless."

"Think of all the guys who'll jack off to you. That doesn't sound like filler to me."

"No, I guess there's that."

"Oh, and bring your pipe and some rocks. I think I'll have a taste. And wake Kitten up. I got something planned for her, too."

"Fine."

Guy looked up at the moon. Nice night. Cold but invigorating. Perfect for having some fun with his girls.

RUSSELL

Stupid bitch, Russell thought as he trudged forward. He kicked a twig out of his path. Why'd she have to go off on her own? Yeah, it was sort of his fault for leading Bigfoot to her. And yeah, it was his fault for not realizing there were drugs in the bag and the hairy fucker wanted meth so badly it would knock down the forest to get to it. But still, how was he supposed to know all that until after the fact?

Fuck it. She made her choice. If it wakes up and manages to find her, then it is what it is. Just like if it comes to and gets a hold of me, then it's my own damn fault, aint' it? No one's going to cry over my dismembered body.

Except maybe mom.

The thought of her brought him out of the surreal haze of the evening and back into the reality that was his life before all this craziness went down. He now had enough money on his back to finish mom's chemo treatments. Hell, he might have enough left over to pack up his stuff and leave. In a way, he had to. The Sheriff had no doubt identified Mickey's truck by now. Body, too. That fucker Stanger was always harassing Mickey and him. Pulling them over. Trying to find any excuse he could to search their cars. Never worked, though.

So he's had to have told the Sheriff Russell was the partner. They'd want to pick him up. Bring him in. Maybe they'd pin the murders on him. He was an accessory at the very least. And they had his shotgun with his prints…

Yeah, they'd pin it on him. No doubt now. His luck, life in prison.

Well, you're truly fucked, aren't you, Russell thought. So pay mom's freight and bug out town while they're still distracted with Bigfoot and all.

Sure thing. Just need to make it out of the woods.

Russell stopped for a moment and looked around. Everything looked exactly the same. He knew Bigfoot was behind him. But ahead of him? *Shit*, he thought he would have hit the Loop by now. He just hoped he wasn't walking in one big circle. He remembered hearing stories about people doing that. The idea made him slightly queasy.

"Well looky what we've got here."

Russell froze as a gun cocked to his right. Slightly queasy became full on queasy in a microsecond. He shifted his head enough to catch a man in a Sheriff's Department uniform pointing a .38 at the side of his head.

"Easy, asshole," the deputy said. "No sudden moves."

Shit, Russell thought. He wondered if he could overwhelm him. Somehow get the gun away and take off.

"What'd you find?"

A different voice. Somewhere behind Russell. Feet approached. So much for overwhelming and running away.

The second man came around and stood in front of him Russell. Another Sheriff's Deputy. The name tag read BETTS. He reeked of beer.

"Found me the guy Stanger was talking about. The partner of that dead guy at the house."

"There were a bunch of dead guys at the house, Pronger."

"The dead drug dealer."

"Oh, yeah." Betts stepped closer. "Russell, right? Russell O'Brien."

"That'd be the one." Pronger circled around and stood next to Betts, barrel a few inches from Russell's face. "Fits the description and all. He's the one that went running off into the woods when the shooting started."

Fuck, Russell thought. They knew his name and description and had already connected him to fleeing the scene. Son of a bitch times a thousand.

"Guess he got himself lost in the woods," Betts said.

"No shit." Pronger smirked. "You think he meant to come back the way he started?"

Back the way I started? Russell felt like someone had just kicked him in the balls. Managed to escape Bigfoot only to walk right back into the waiting arms of the Sheriff. Fucking cursed.

"Life's a bitch, ain't it?" Pronger said. "Sheriff's going to be real happy to see you."

"Not as much as Bigfoot."

They chuckled.

Russell didn't get the joke. "What do you mean happy to see Bigfoot?"

"Who said you get to ask questions, asshole?" Betts said. "By the way, where is the big hairy bastard?"

Russell motioned his head over his shoulder. "Back there sleeping. Why don't you go wake it up?"

"Smart ass," Betts said. "Should pistol whip your ass."

"I'm not joking. It's back there sleeping. Hit the wall after that meth rage."

Pronger rose up on his toes and peered over Russell's shoulder like he'd be able to see the creature out there in the dark. "Seriously? It's sleeping?"

"Yeah. Knocked the fuck out. Chased me up a tree. That's how I got all turned around."

Betts smiled and looked at Pronger. "Guess it's our lucky night." Then he shifted back to Russell. "But not yours."

No, it's not. "So, you two are looking for it?"

"Sheriff wants to get his hands on it." Pronger said. "How far back is it?"

Russell shrugged and wondered why the Sheriff would want to get anywhere near the thing. Then he realized he probably wanted to make money off it. Maybe there was a way out of this after all. "About a ten minute walk. Don't know how long it'll be out for. Might want to go kill it while you've got the advantage."

Pronger licked his lips. "Maybe we should."

"What about this asshole?" Betts said.

"Take him with us."

"No fucking way," Russell said. "I ain't going anywhere near that thing again."

Pronger's lips tightened and he pressed the barrel against Russell's forehead. "Who said you got a choice?"

"You'll have to fucking kill me."

"That can be arranged."

Russell swallowed and gritted his teeth but he wasn't going to yield. He'd rather die with a bullet in his head than go back there and get his arms torn out. No way he was dying like Mickey.

"Sheriff wants to take care of it, remember," Betts said. "We take care of it, he might get pissed off."

Pronger didn't move the gun. Kept staring into Russell's eyes. "Yeah, don't want to piss the Sheriff off. Tends to do… crazy things sometimes. He's already pretty excited over all this. Can't wait to see what he does when we bring old Russell to him."

"Probably give him the Wheezy treatment."

Pronger winced. "Hope not. *I* even felt bad for Wheezy."

Russell licked his lips. He could feel sweat on his palms. "What about Bigfoot?"

"Betts is right. Got to leave the monster to the Sheriff. He's got a big old plan for it. Can't ruin it."

"Yep. We didn't lay all that meth out for nothing."

"Meth?" Russell's hands started shaking at his sides. "You put meth out?"

"Made a trail from the cabin all the way out here." Betts clapped his hands. "Best way to catch a drug addict is to lead him to the product, right?"

Fuck, fuck, fuck, Russell thought. He flexed his hands into fists and then opened and then closed. Over and over. It wouldn't be much longer. It would catch the scent. The sweet smell of bliss would wake its ass up. And then it would be on the warpath again. Coming straight this way. Holy shit!

"Lead him to a death trap," Pronger said. He lowered the .38 and grabbed Russell by the elbow. "How about we go see the Sheriff before all the fireworks start?"

Betts took him by the other elbow. "Yeah, need to get you out of the way before the real fun begins."

"This is a bad idea," Russell said, trying to keep his feet planted. Both men were surprisingly strong, though, and pulled him forward without much trouble.

"Sure you'd say that," Pronger said.

"No, you don't understand. That thing will kill us all."

"Nah. It'll walk right into the middle of our trap and we'll put it down nice and easy."

"Like you did the first time?"

Betts turned and rammed a left hook into his stomach. Russell folded and coughed. Bile burned his throat. Felt like a mule had kicked him.

"We were caught off guard," Betts said. "Most of us shot wide and wild. It got lucky."

They resumed walking. Russell coughed some more. His eyes watered. Nauseous and scared. His elbows ached where Pronger and Betts held him in a death grip. He wanted to quit all together. Make them drag him back to the cabin. But fear of Bigfoot waking up and finding the newly laid meth trail kept him walking. He didn't want to be anywhere near it when that happened. No matter what the Sheriff did, Russell would rather deal with him than it.

"You don't need to worry about it," Pronger said, as if reading his mind. "You'll be nice and safe from Bigfoot. The Sheriff is the one you got to worry about. I saw what happened to Wheezy. Put it this way, you get the same treatment, you'll never be the same again."

After tonight, Russell thought, *I know I'll never be the same again.* He just hoped he survived to see another day.

GABE

"So Betts and Pronger are out in the woods laying a trail of meth back to here?" Stanger said, rubbing the back of his neck. "And we ain't got an armored truck to trap Bigfoot in."

Gabe had just finished shooting his wad when Stanger and Lyle pulled back up. He managed to snort another pinch before they found him standing behind the cabin, staring at the trees.

"Yeah, that's how it is." Gabe rubbed his balls through his pants. Ached pretty badly. Could use another round of stroking. "So we lure it back here and kill it instead."

"I don't know, Sheriff," Lyle said. "I don't like this. Feels wrong."

Gabe winced. Lyle was such a pussy sometimes. He'd said the same thing with Wheezy. "Gee, Sheriff, I don't like this. Feels wrong." Well, *he'd* been wrong then and he's wrong now.

Stop thinking about it, Gabe told himself. The thoughts were only getting the juices flowing again and he didn't want to deal with Lyle and a growing hard-on and a pair of aching balls at the same time. Just too damn…weird.

"I hate to say, it," Stanger said, "But I kind of agree with Lyle. This feels off somehow. Like we're desperate."

Anger pulsed through Gabe's forearms. Not Stanger. Anyone but Stanger.

"You think we should pack up and leave?" Gabe rounded on Stanger. "What if it gets its hands on some innocent civilians? What if it rips a kid in two?"

Stanger held up his hands. "Easy. I'm not saying we don't take care of it."

"Then what are you saying?"

"That leaving a bunch of meth for it to follow might not be

the best idea. I mean, it has a sense of smell and it knows the house it was getting fed at. We could have made a pile right here and it would have found its way back."

"I see." Gabe shook his head. "You don't understand how this shit works. You think letting it grow into another fiend rage is the way to do it. Cock tease it instead of giving it a taste along the way."

"No—"

"Yes because if you knew, you'd know the more it gobbles up on the way back here, the less aggressive it'll be. Aggressive still, but not in a fucking fiend rage."

"Sheriff—"

"You apparently didn't see the way it took a couple of shotgun blasts. So let me ask you this: which Bigfoot do you want to deal with? Drugged-up and happy monkey or drug-withdrawal and batshit crazy monkey?"

"Drugged-up and happy." Stanger placed his hands on his hips and sighed. "I thought meth made people aggressive, though."

"It's a bi-product. Depends on the personality. What it really does is boost the confidence. Makes you feel like you can take on the world." Or a big legendary ape.

"Take on the world, huh." Lyle snorted a laugh. "Maybe we should take some before Bigfoot shows up. Know I could use a little more confidence."

You could, could you? Gabe thought. *Not a bad idea, Lyle.*

He did want everyone sharp and focused. Wanted them to shoot straight and not all over creation because their hands were shaking like a bunch of epileptics.

"Come over here." Gabe headed to the nearest car. He pulled out his last baggie of meth and sprinkled the pieces on the hood. Then he drew his sidearm and held it by the barrel and tapped the pieces into grainy chunks.

"Sheriff, what the hell are you doing?" Stanger said.

"Extraordinary times call for extraordinary measures." Gabe turned to them. "Lyle's right, we all need a shot of confidence."

"You can't be serious."

"I am. Deadly serious."

Lyle waved his arms. "I was just joking."

"Joking, sure. But you stumbled onto the truth. When that fucking thing comes out of the trees, we need to be Johnny on the spot. Focused and mean and fail proof. I think we need to use the weapon of our enemy to our advantage in this case."

"Ain't doing it," Stanger said.

"This isn't a request." Gabe cocked the gun.

"Or what, you're going to shoot me? Me? Have you lost your mind?"

"I'm not going to shoot you." Gabe leveled the barrel at Lyle's forehead. "I'll shoot him."

"Ah, fuck, Sheriff," Lyle said.

Stanger held up a hand for calm. "Go easy."

"Snort a pinch then." Gabe pointed at the chunks. "Now."

Stanger licked his lips and looked at the meth for a second. "You're not going to kill Lyle."

"I'm so fucking serious I'll kill both of you. If I can't trust you, I don't want you around."

"Let us leave then."

"Can't do that either."

"Why not?"

Gabe reached out and took a pinch and snorted it fast. He howled and stomped his foot. Then he rubbed his growing erection. "Because you're all fucking accessories now."

"Jesus Christ," Stanger said. "You've been snorting the entire time we've been gone, haven't you?"

"Fuckin' A right," Gabe howled again and pushed the barrel into Lyle's ear. Lyle whined. "And I don't like your tone, Deputy."

"You're nuts. I always knew you were sort of nuts but you're actually fucking nuts."

Gabe laughed and snorted another pinch and jammed the barrel into Lyle's ear so hard he cried and tried to jerk away. Gabe ceased the movement by whipping the barrel again the side of Lyle's head. Blood ran from a three inch cut across his temple. He swayed and then dropped to a knee and pushed his hand against the fresh wound.

THE AMATEURS

By the time Bunny dragged Kitten out of the tent and half-carried her toward Guy, his bladder was on the verge of exploding. He couldn't wait for them anymore. Couldn't hold it while watching Bunny death-grip Kitten's waist with her left arm while clenching the wrist of the right arm wrapped behind her neck.

"Come on, bitch," Bunny said, "You've got more energy than that."

Kitten's head lolled and her eyes blinked hard and in slow-motion.

Fuck this, Guy thought and shuffled over to them. "Get her on her knees."

Bunny let go and Kitten hit the ground like a dead body. No sound. No movement.

Guy stood over her, holding his groin, pee-pee dancing. "Camera ready?"

"Yeah."

"Start rolling."

Bunny knelt to the side and focused the camera. "It's hard to get all of her and your dick in the shot."

Damn it, he thought. He nudged Kitten's shoulder with his foot. "Kitten, it's time for the shower scene. Come on, be a pro and rally. We need this shot."

"Do it with Bunny." The voice was mumbled, barely audible. But it was there. And there was energy in it, just like Bunny had said while getting her ass this far out of the tent.

Guy gritted his teeth. "Bunny did the anal scene. Did all the scenes today because your ass was in a dope haze. Now it's time to pull you weight. If not, no money and no more crank."

Kitten moved. Not slow. She rolled onto her ass and pulled

her legs in so they crossed, Indian-style. She looked up his dick into Guy's eyes. They were soft but narrow. Dirt crossed diagonally from her right shoulder across her tiny breasts. Looked liked claw marks in the moonlight.

"You wouldn't." Her voice was ice.

"Oh, you fucking bet I would." Man did he want to piss on her. Piss on her right now. But he needed it to look good. Need to keep it professional, not personal. "This isn't crank welfare. You want your taste, you need to put in time. Want your money, you need to earn it. Time to earn it."

She crossed her arms. Defiant. "I want a taste now then."

What the fuck side of the bed did this bitch wake up on? First she's almost in a drug coma. Hell, she's almost dead. Now she's dictating the rules of their business arrangement. Fuck that.

But Guy had to piss. Piss like twenty racehorses.

"Hurry the fuck up and take a hit then."

Kitten smiled. Mocking. She took her pipe from Bunny. Preloaded with rocks. She sparked up and inhaled and moaned. Orgasm moaned. She took another.

"Hey, ones enough for now," Guy said, shifting his weight back and forth between the balls of his feet. "I need to film this."

"Fine." Smoke rose and then drifted away on the light breeze. She handed her pipe to Bunny. "Ready when you are."

A gunshot echoed around them.

"I knew I heard gunshots earlier," Bunny said. "That's why a dreamt it."

"Probably someone drunk and shooting in the air." Guy looked over at Bunny, who was taking her own hit. "Hey, are you rolling?"

Bunny coughed and set the pipe down and picked up the camera. "I am now."

Fuckers. "Okay. Kitten, try to push those itty bitty tits together. And look up at me."

Kitten did. Even smiled at him.

Another gunshot.

"Wonder what's going on," Kitten said.

"Who gives a shit," Guy said. "Sounds like a pistol. Probably shooting beer bottles or something. Now let's do this."

"I thought I didn't want to get peed on," Bunny said. "Figured it was a sad statement on life. But this is worse, filming it. Like I'm not even living a life. Like I don't even exist."

"Will you shut the fuck up and just record!"

"Recording."

Guy looked down at Kitten. Down at her smiling face and tiny breasts. Down at her gaunt neck and bony shoulders. And started to piss.

It smelled it. Smelled it on the wind. Not much. Just the faintest scent. But it was enough.

Bigfoot blinked. It's eyes shifted. Back and forth. Back and forth. The scent. It had it. Had it on the wind. Wanted it. Wanted to find it.

It rocked to its side and pushed up to its knees. It moaned. But it didn't stop. It moved to its feet. Straightened up. Moaned some more and rubbed its wounds. Blood still seeped from its chest and arms. Not as bad. But the pain…

Needed more. Need to follow the scent on the wind.

Bigfoot trudged forward, looking for food.

MANNY

"So you were camping by yourself?" Manny said in a whisper.

A twig crunched under Seph's foot. The sound echoed around them. Manny winced reflexively. She had just given them away. If this were a game of life and death, they'd be caught, maybe dead. If they were being tracked, the hounds would be on them. But nothing like that happened.

Because it's not that kind of situation, he thought. *We're not humping through enemy territory or evading an aggressor force. We're just hiking to my home. Bigfoot wanted drugs. Simple as that. Relax already.*

"Yeah, I was. I don't want to talk about it though."

"Fair enough."

They walked for a few seconds without exchanging another word. Manny was relieved for the reprieve. For the first few minutes, Seph had done nothing but explain over and over how Russell had led Bigfoot right to her. Manny didn't interrupt, letting it pour out of her like water from a fire hose. He wouldn't point out how Russell hadn't done anything malicious. Stupid, yes, but he hadn't meant to involve her. If Manny had said something like that, he knew he'd be enemy number one by proximity. He couldn't blame her for feeling that way. After all, she'd been peacefully camping. Drinking beers and sitting by a fire. Next thing she knew, there was a panicked man and a wild beast ripping through her world. Nope, couldn't blame her at all.

But he couldn't blame this idiot Russell either. Yeah, he'd had a bag full of drug money. And yeah, there'd been baggies of meth in there that Bigfoot had caught the scent of. Just a shitty situation all around. He wouldn't pass judgment. Not yet at least. In the end, what was gained from the finger pointing? Nothing. A big waste of time. What mattered was making it home and seeing the sunrise without any other complications. He wished Seph understood that. He wasn't about to explain it.

"You're a Marine right?" Seph said.

The question forced his head to cock at an unnatural angle. Like a dog hearing a mysterious sound for the first time. How'd she know? He didn't have visible tattoos of an E.G.A. or a bulldog wearing a Smokey Bear. No Semper Fi shirt either.

"Yes," he said. "What gave it away?"

"The haircut." Her voice was soft. Almost mischievous.

Manny thought, *Maybe*. He forgot his skin close high and tight stood out like a hooker in church.

She said Marine, though. Plenty of military personnel had similar haircuts across all branches of the services. She could have easily guessed Army or (heaven forbid) a squared away squid. But she didn't. She zeroed in on him with the precision of…well, a sniper.

"What made you say Marine?"

"I don't understand."

"I keep my hair like this because anything longer and I feel like a hippie." Manny hated hippies almost as much as cops. "But that's not what gave me away. Why Marine?"

"Honestly?"

"Absolutely."

She chuckled for a second and then said, "You blouse your pants with boot bands."

Manny smiled but didn't look at her. Instead, he proceeded into the night, pine needles crunching under his boots. Yep, she nailed him. Another old habit. He bloused the bottom of his cargo pants with boot bands instead of tucking them in. Marine's don't tuck. Tucking's for Army pussies.

"Well done," he said. "I assume you or someone you know is a Marine." Manny knew she wasn't based on her outdoor skills thus far but figured why insult her with a verbal assumption.

"My dad was."

"Was? I'm guessing he's passed on." Because once a Marine, always a Marine.

"You guess correct."

"I'm sorry for your loss."

"Long time ago." Seph waved her hands back and forth. "It was a long time ago. But thank you."

"Sure." Manny focused on the direction they were walking. He took his bearings, making sure they still headed south-southwest toward the Loop and his house. "What was his M.O.S.?"

"His what?"

"What did he do? Infantry? Artillery?"

"Force Recon."

"Oooh-rah."

"What about you?"

"Sniper."

She was silent a moment. Manny wondered if he'd scared her with his answer. Why not? It was a scary answer.

"Makes sense," Seph said after a few more steps of silence.

Manny smirked. "That's obvious too?"

"No but with all the crazy shit that's happened tonight I asked for help."

"I don't follow."

"When I was in that tree with that asshole Russell, I silently prayed for help. I asked God to protect me. And now I'm walking through the woods with a Marine sniper. I mean any Marine would work but a sniper…well, I can't imagine what would be better protection against Bigfoot. A sure shot's nice to have in your hip pocket."

Yeah, if you can still shoot, Manny thought and bit his bottom lip, drawing blood. Actually the better question was if he could still kill?

"Glad to be of service," he said. "But let's hope it doesn't come to something like that."

"Amen."

A gunshot ripped the night. Manny lowered to one knee and motioned for Seph to do the same. She did. The echo of the shot continued for another second. Pistol. Probably a .38 or .357 shooting non-magnum loads.

A cop's gun, he thought.

Maybe the Sheriff had gotten the beast. Manny shook his head at the thought. No way. Not with a handgun. Not even with one at close range.

So who's that son of a bitch shooting then?

"What direction was that?" Seph said.

"Toward the side of the Loop where all this shit started." Manny listened, waiting to hear cheers or screams or something. Only there wasn't anything. Not even the rustle of branches in the breeze.

Another gunshot. Same as before. Exact same echo, too. Fired in the same position near the cabin on the Loop which had been the home of those idiot meth cookers.

Two shots two minutes apart. Same gun. No screams.

Deliberate, Manny thought. His experience with deliberate and well-paced shots all boiled down to the same explanation: execution.

"What's going on?" Seph said.

I don't want to answer that right now. "Sounds like something may be getting resolved."

"For the better."

"I'm pretty sure that isn't what's happening."

"I don't like any of this."

Manny broke his concentration and turned his head toward Seph. Dried blood covered her forehead and eyebrows. Her eyes stared into the darkness. She nibbled her lower lip. He reached out with his left hand but she didn't seem to notice.

"We're going to be okay."

Seph let go of the darkness and shifted to him. She smiled lightly at his hand and took it in hers and squeezed. "Thank you."

"How about we just wait here a second and listen? Seems safer than walking around right now. Just in case."

She nodded. "Just in case."

RUSSELL/GABE

The first gunshot froze Pronger and Betts in their tracks. Russell's momentum carried him forward a few inches even as he wondered what the hell else could go wrong tonight. Then the deputies snapped him back. He managed to keep his feet even though he stood on rubbery legs. It helped they had hands firmly cupped under each of his armpits.

"That sounded like a revolver," Pronger said. "Dead ahead."

Poor choice of words, Russell thought and figured it was safe to say he was officially cursed. Christ, he just wanted this to end all-fucking-ready.

"Maybe Bigfoot showed back up and the Sheriff got him," Betts said.

"You think we would have heard it growl or something considering the way it was carrying on earlier."

"What else could it be then?"

Russell didn't want to find out. Just wanted to get away from these two idiots while he still had his sk—

Another shot. Same report as before.

"Ah, shit," Pronger said. "That didn't sound good."

Betts licked his lips. "Maybe we should hang back."

That's the smartest thing you've probably ever said, Russell thought. "I'm good with that."

Pronger leaned into Russell's ear. "Shut the fuck up." He leaned out and eyed Betts. "Maybe the Sheriff's in trouble."

"I got a bad feeling." Betts shook his head and kind of marched in place. "You saw how he was waving that gun around earlier."

"Who was waving a gun around?" It came out before Russell could catch himself.

Pronger threw a brick of a fist into his stomach. Pain burst up his torso into his throat and down into his groin. Russell dropped to a knee, coughing.

"I told you to shut the fuck up."

Russell held up a hand in surrender and coughed and spat a mouthful of saliva.

"Maybe he's up their shooting squirrels," Pronger said. "He is an impatient bastard."

"I'll follow your lead but for the record I'm against this."

Pronger nodded. "We'll approach nice and slow and see what's what. Good enough?"

"Yeah, that'll work."

Russell spat another mouthful as they hoisted him back to his feet.

Pronger yanked him forward. "Let's go tough guy."

Where the fuck is everyone? Gabe thought.

He paced around Stanger and Lyle's pussy-ass bodies, scratching his neck. Wanted to fucking kill Bigfoot already but the hairy little fuck was a no show. Probably because Pronger and Betts were out there placing the baggies up their own asses.

Maybe they were a couple of fags, too. He wouldn't be surprised. Surrounded by knob bobbers all this time. Damn surprised he'd been able to do his job this long. But business as usual was over. Stanger and Lyle found that out right quick. So would Pronger and Betts.

IF THEY FUCKING SHOWED UP!!!

He stopped pacing and turned and gazed down at his recently departed deputies. Fucking worthless. Just laying there waiting for the flies and worms to eat them. No damn good to anyone else.

"Because." Gabe lifted his boot and stomped down on Stanger's head. "You." Stomp. "Were." Stomp. "Always." Stomp. "Worthless." Stomp, stomp, stomp.

Gabe breathed hard and stepped away and looked down at his boot. Caked in gore. It was beautiful.

He shifted to Lyle. "And you. So soft and weak." He dropped to his knees in bloody mud at the top of Lyle's head. "With your soft and weak mouth." Gabe reached out and thumbed Lyle's graying bottom lip. "Only thing it was probably good for was blowing truckers."

The words reminded Gabe of Tawny bobbing up and down on his cock. Man, what was with him tonight? He reached down and felt his dick hardening again and knew meth was his Viagra. That and the violence and the blood. Oh, it was all so *sweeeet*. Meth, sex, and blood: his holy trinity.

And Lyle's mouth. Like Tawny's mouth. Soft and ready to received.

"Should have made you suck my cock long ago." Gabe started to pull down his fly. "Never too late."

Behind him he heard movement in the woods. Feet coming down on pine needles. Gabe released his zipper and rose to a squat and scurried behind the cruiser. Listened. More than two feet. Four or six. About fifteen yards deep in the woods.

Hot damn! This shit heightens all the senses!

He side-stepped over to the tree line, gun in a firm two-handed grip. Stopped. Listened. Could hear whispering but couldn't distinguish what was said. No Bigfoot for sure.

Maybe Betts and Pronger. But why were they whispering?

Because they're conspiring faggots. Probably see the bodies and are planning how to ambush me.

Gabe slowly and quietly cocked his gun.

Guess we'll see real soon who gets ambushed, he thought.

"Holy shit," Betts whispered.

"Stanger and Lyle." Pronger had his gun raised in front of him. "He killed them both."

They were still a few feet from the tree line but had a clear view of the carnage. Russell didn't know who either one of them were but the sight still forced him to choke down a gullet full of bile. Then out of nowhere he thought of Homer Simpson.

Russell stifled a laugh. He'd recently watched *The Simpsons Movie* with his mom. For some reason, the scene where Bart is forced to stand naked in public as punishment after skateboarding bare-assed through town popped into his mind now. Near the end of the scene, Homer walks up to his son. Bart declares it's the worst day of his life. And Homer, in his infinite wisdom, says, "Worst day so far."

Isn't that just the perfect description of this fucking day? Russell thought and gnawed on his cheeks to keep from laughing hysterically. Worst day so far indeed.

"He killed them," Betts said. "Holy shit he killed them."

"We don't know that."

"What else could have happened? You think Bigfoot managed to shoot them? Last time I checked that fucking thing was ripping people's arms out, not popping caps in them."

"All I'm saying is we don't know—"

"You saw him, man. You saw the look in his eye when he threatened us. *Us.*"

Russell had chased thoughts of Homer and Bart away. Now he focused on Pronger. The deputy seemed lost. Not sure what to do next, focusing on the bodies and moving his mouth as if ready to say something but unable to find the words. Russell understood that feeling pretty well. Felt the same way when Mickey was torn to pieces in front of him.

Life altering reality's a real bitch, huh? Russell thought. Relief sparkled in the corner of his eye. At least he didn't have to worry about the Sheriff and the Wheezy treatment anymore. No way these two would go anywhere near the bastard after this.

"What's all this about threats and killing?"

Russell's blood turned to ice. He knew the voice. Right behind them.

"Hi, Sheriff," Pronger said, not moving.

"Cut the shit and turn around real slow. All three of you."

Russell waited until Pronger and Betts moved, inch by inch, before he joined them. When they completed the one-eighty, they found the Sheriff in a wide stance holding a pistol in a double-grip. Cocked.

Russell heard Homer's words again in his head but there was no urge to laugh this time. Nope, none at all. He looked into the Sheriff's eyes and knew. Knew all too well. He'd seen the same look many times in the mirror. The euphoria. The paranoia. The rage. All dancing rings around each other. The motherfucker was high on crank.

Betts held up his hands. "Easy, Sheriff."

"You take easy and shove it up your dick. What's going on here?"

"We just finished laying the trail like you told us to." Pronger pointed at Russell. "And we came across him. He's Mickey's partner."

Russell wanted to shrink to the size of an ant. The Sheriff focused all that meth fog right on him. It was like his eyes were laser guided bombs.

"Mickey's partner?" he said.

"Yeah," Pronger said. "We knew you'd want to deal with him."

"Mickey's partner, huh?" The Sheriff nodded and released the two-handed grip and rubbed his crotch with is left hand. "Yeah, I want to deal with him."

Oh, no, Russell thought.

"So we're cool?" Pronger said.

The Sheriff never took his eyes off Russell. "I should ask you the same question."

Pronger shrugged. "Figure you had your reasons."

"You're damn right I did."

Betts cleared his throat. "I don't mean to push—" Pronger tried to shoosh him. "—but can you tell us what they did."

"Sure I can." Now he broke his stare and shifted to Betts. "They failed to follow orders."

"They—"

"WERE INSUBORDINATE!"

It was like he shot all three of them. Russell winced and both deputies stepped back as if gut shot.

"Are you being insubordinate, Betts?"

"No, Sheriff. Not at all." Voice desperate. High. Pleading. "Just wanted to be sure."

"You doubting my judgment?"

Pronger stepped forward, hand out. "He's just stupid."

Russell looked at Betts. He licked his lips but was smart enough to hold his tongue. Looked back to the Sheriff. A smile sprouted under those crazy eyes.

"Stupid is right." The Sheriff howled. Howled at the fucking moon like a wolf. "Always fucking stupid. But you're loyal, Betts. Right?"

"Y-y-yes."

"And you, too, Pronger? Loyal? Not like Stanger and Lyle."

"You know it, Sheriff."

"Good, good." The Sheriff pointed the barrel at the back of the cabin. "Take him up there by the cruiser. I'll deal with him there."

Fuck me, Russell thought, knowing there was a bullet with his name on it. So that's the Wheezy treatment, huh? Shot in the head and buried in a shallow grave somewhere. Son of a bitch.

The Sheriff slapped his thigh with his free hand. "Chop, chop. Let's move."

He blew past them and stomped toward the cruiser. When he was a few feet away, Betts turned to Pronger and whispered, "We need to get the hell out of here."

"Shut up." Pronger watched the Sheriff. "He's lost it. If we're not smart, we'll end up the same as Stanger and Lyle."

"But—"

"Quiet."

Betts did as commanded and the two dragged Russell out of the woods and over to the cruiser. With every step, Russell's grip on life slipped. The wild, crazed eyes of the Sheriff bore into Russell's forehead. Hungry. Ready for blood. More blood.

God save my mom, Russell thought. It was the only thing he could think. He was not a praying man. Not a religious man. But he couldn't form any other words. *God save my mom*.

"Bring that bitch right over here."

Betts and Pronger complied. They walked Russell to the hood and pushed him against the front end and stepped back. Gabe circled the car, looking at the back of Russell's head until he came back around and faced him. The little shit was quivering. Eyes averted. Staring at dirt and ants.

Damn right.

"Look at me."

Russell didn't comply.

"I'll shoot your dick off."

The head raised enough for them to make eye contact. Scared shitless.

Gabe reached down and grabbed his hard-on. Rock solid and ready to go. He needed the satisfaction of blood. Needed the taste of violence again. But what to do with this little bitch?

The Wheezy treatment of course. Only taken up a notch or two.

"Remember Wheezy?" Gabe said. Betts and Pronger nodded. They stood off to the side. Almost like they positioned themselves to make a run for the driveway.

Can't have that.

"I think he's earned the same treatment."

They nodded again but then paused. They looked at each other a moment before turning back to him. Gabe already knew the question. Who was going to do it? There wasn't a homeless guy who'd do anything for fifty bucks here this time. Gabe would have to take matters into his own hands.

"I know, I know. Who's going to do the deed?" Gabe reached up and undid the top button of his shirt. "Guess I'll take the first go." He undid another button. "You two get to hold him down."

Betts and Pronger look at each other again. Nervous. Fucking cunts. Was there anyone he could trust anymore?

Russell understood. All too well. Both hands were braced palms down on the hood. He was ready to fight if he had to. To kick and scream. Fuck yeah! The desperation only got Gabe that much more excited.

"We thought you would want to handle this down at the jail." Pronger's Adam's apple bobbed. "We could get another bum—"

"Nah." Gabe finished off the last button and pulled one arm free of a sleeve. "We'll do it right here." He switched gun hands and pulled the other arm out. "Now hold that bitch down."

Pronger and Betts didn't move. Instead, they only stared at Russell. Son of a bitch if they didn't look sorry.

Enough of this shit, Gabe thought and leveled the gun at Pronger's head. "You fucking deaf all of the sudden?"

"No, Sheriff."

"What about you, Betts?"

"No."

"Then hold him down already."

Betts and Pronger walked over to Russell and grabbed each arm and spun him around. Then bent him over the hood and pinned his shoulders down. With their other hands, they mashed his face into cold metal.

Gabe saw the pack then, rising up on Russell's back like a camel hump. "What's in the bag?"

Pronger stammered before saying, "We forgot to search it."

For fuck's sake, Gabe thought but then relented. Maybe it was a blessing. If there was meth in there, these two idiots would have added it to the Bigfoot trail. Instead, they'd failed to search their prisoner and may have brought him a bagful of heaven.

"Take it off."

They did.

"Toss it over here."

They did and resumed holding the little bitch down.

Gabe squatted and unzipped the bag with his free hand and peeked. He had to fight not to howl. Better than heaven. This fucking bag could buy him the week of a lifetime in Vegas. Hookers, blow, crank, and whatever else he'd fantasized about and hadn't indulged in yet. A dwarf. Yeah, he'd wanted to try one. Maybe set up a gang-bang. The possibilities made him shiver.

"You okay, Sheriff?"

"Yeah." He zipped the bag and pushed it to the side and rose. "Just some more meth."

Russell groaned.

Gabe smiled. Yeah, you're going to groan all right.

"Let's get this nasty business settled."

***

Russell wanted to die. He thought he didn't. Though if he could survive Mickey's assassination needs and Bigfoot's drug-crazed rampage he was golden. Everything wine and roses and a bag full of money for mom's treatments and his early retirement. Until these two dipshits had found him. Even then, he figured he might make it out alive. Maybe roughed up but things seemed to be working out no matter how fucked up they were. Mickey had gotten ripped to pieces, not him. Bigfoot had been chasing the meth in his bag, not him. When they saw the two murdered deputies, he knew for sure he'd make it out. No way they'd take him to the Sheriff. Hell, no way they'd go to the Sheriff ever again for anything.

Then that son of a bitch ambushed them. Now here he was, bent over the hood of a police car. The Sheriff, somewhere behind him, stroking a meth hard-on and pumping himself up to rape him.

Worst day so far, he thought. Not laughing now. No, it was going to get far worse real quick. He wished he and Mickey could go back and switch places.

A hand tugged at his belt. He could feel hot breath on his ear. He smelled whiskey.

"Ever been gored by a rhino?" Russell winced as he felt his thighs exposed to the cool air. "Ever had your shithole turned inside out?" Now the air smacked his bare ass. He shivered against his will. The Sheriff whistled behind him. "Look at that. Pale and flat. Guess it'll do though."

God save my mom, Russell thought and closed his eyes. *Please kill me.*

A belt buckle jingled free behind him. Pants sliding down against legs. Another whistle.

"I'd show you this, Russell, but I don't want you anymore scared than you already are. Let's just say I'm at attention and your ass is ready for inspection."

Please kill me.

Feet shuffled closer. He could feel the tip of the Sheriff's dick against his right cheek. The barrel of the Sheriff's gun pushed against the back of his head.

"Hmmm."

"What's the matter, Sheriff?" Betts said.

Please kill all of them, too.

"Only got the one free hand," the Sheriff said. "And I like the idea of keeping the gun pushed into his skull while I do it…Tell you what. Each of you grab an ass cheek and spread them apart so I can get up in there."

Don't kill me God, he thought. *Keep me alive and let me kill every single one of these motherfuckers.*

THE AMATEURS

Guy inhaled a solid lungful and smiled, taking it all in. The moon. The cool steady breeze. An owl hooting. Kittens mouth sliding up and down on his cock. Perfect.

He exhaled and passed the pipe to Kitten. She pulled his dick from her mouth, inhaled, and went right back to blowing him. Smoke escaped her mouth, the warmth causing him to shiver. His balls tightened. She sensed it and probed his asshole with a finger.

"Not too much," he said. "I don't want to come yet."

She complied, massaging the outer rim instead of plunging in. Guy sighed and took another hit. Bunny shifted around on the ground, knocked the fuck out. She'd hit it pretty hard after the shower scene. The whole thing, the pissing, the moaning, seemed to have depressed her beyond her normal melancholy self. So much she would talk about it…which was definitely not in her character. It was like her and Kitten switched personalities. Bunny wanted to do nothing more than smoke and sleep. Kitten wanted nothing more than to eat his cock. It was like the piss had flipped some lustful switch in her body. Whatever it was, Guy wasn't complaining.

He wanted it on film, of course. He made Bunny set up the tripod before she drifted off to Never Never Land. So the camera stood a foot feet away, recording Kitten in close-up and she bobbed away.

A blood-curdling scream cut the night air. Kitten let go and turned toward it, dragging her teeth a little along the way.

"Ouch," Guy said. "Careful."

"Did you hear that?"

"Yeah, hard to miss."

Another scream. And another. Male by the sound of it.

"Sounds like the poor guy's being tortured."

"Nah," Guy said. "You know what that sounds like?"
"What?" She was still looking off into the darkness.
"Sounds like the guy's getting railed. Hard."
She turned to him now. "That's a fucked up thing to say."
"It's true. Know how I know that?"
Kitten didn't say anything.
"You sounded just like that when I popped your cherry. Remember that? You screamed bloody murder."
"You weren't exactly gentle."
Guy shrugged. "I am what I am." He put his hand on top of her head and guided it back toward his dick. "Now let's ignore that little distraction." Kitten smirked but then opened her mouth and went back to work. "That's good."

A few minutes passed. The screams didn't let up. Kitten didn't either. Guy kind of dug it. The screams. Kitten got crazy on him. Her finger massaging his asshole. It was surreal. But cool.

"Faster," he said. "And go ahead and push that finger in. I think I'm going to come."

Again she complied. The finger went in. Guy arched his back and thrust his pelvis toward her face. He closed his eyes and rocked his head back and sucked in the moonlight.

And then there were muffled screams. Kitten stopped blowing him. Her finger slid out of his ass. He could still feel the inside of her mouth but she'd stopped all back and forth motion for some fucking reason.

"What the fuck?" Guy said and rocked his head forward and opened his eyes.

He saw nothing but hair. Some of it was matted with blood. Then the stench hit him. Shit, must, earth. Guy didn't look up, though. Something told him not to. Instead, he looked down and found two giant hands, palms pressed against both sides of Kitten's head like a vice.

It grunted. Guy understood what it meant. Look up, it said. Look at me.

He did, his eyes drifting up the torso. It looked down at him, eyes full of pain and hunger. Eyes full of fury.

It roared and Guy screamed and Kitten wailed around his

cock. Then its arms flexed and Kitten's wails stopped. Hot fluid and chunks of something splattered Guy's stomach. He looked down to find the thing's hands now touching, pieces of Kitten's head and hair still pressed between them.

Guy backed away. Rather easily. Then he realized his was pissing blood. No, he wasn't pissing. He looked down and found the blood-jutting from the stump that was now his dick.

Now the pain came, spreading out in all directions in his body from his groin. He screamed and cupped his stump and ran. He made it a few feet and tripped over the tripod and camera. He hit the ground next to Bunny. Rolled onto his back.

It stood over him. It raised its foot over Guy's head. It roared and its foot crashed down toward him, blocking out all light. And all of Guy's pain stopped.

MANNY

They'd been sitting there in the dark for ten minutes when Seph said, "I think we can risk walking. What do you think?"

Manny started to nod when a man's scream ripped the air. One long agonizing scream. Seph jumped next to him and he squeezed her hand to remind her he was there.

No other screams followed. Manny locked in on the direction it emanated from based on the echo and dissipation. Not far. Half a mile. Somewhere on the Loop—

The cabin, he thought. The gunshots, the scream. All coming from the same damn place.

"I want to go home." Her voice was low and resigned.

"Someone's in trouble."

"Whoever it is is probably dead."

Manny looked at her. The moonlight had all but disappeared yet he could still see the fear creasing the skin around her eyes and mouth. He wanted to leave, too. Wanted to pretend he hadn't heard that tortured wail. But he couldn't. Someone was in trouble and he might be the only one who could do anything about it.

"Hey." Manny ran his thumb across her knuckles until she focused on him. "I have to go see if I can help."

"What about me?"

"If you stay with me, you'll be safe but I won't make you go."

"What if going gets us both killed?"

"So you'd let whoever that was suffer?"

She wiped away a tear. "That's a hell of a thing to say."

"You understand what I mean, though. I can't ignore it."

She nodded. "I just don't want to go."

"Neither do I."

Seph smirked. "At least we agree on that."

Manny let go of her hand. "We'll approach slow. With the scope I'll be able to survey from far enough away as not to put us in an indefensible position."

"What if you see something bad?"

"There's a lot more I can do with this scope and rifle than just observe." Manny hoped he could back those words up. "We won't have to get close."

That seemed to ease the fear a bit. "Okay."

"All right then. Let's go. Nice and slow and quiet."

The screams continued the entire way. At one point, when they were fairly close, Manny swore he heard two different guys screaming, maybe even the roar of the beast but chalked it up to an echo. The screaming and the grunts and howling from the cabin was just too loud to discern anything else that might be going on around them. They all came from in front of them. He was sure of that.

Manny heard the grunts before Seph. When she did after a few more steps, she said it sounded like an animal. Manny knew better but didn't say. When they grew a little closer, the screams faded to feeble sobs. Barely noticeable between the grunts. Neither one said anything about those.

He glassed the woods ahead but could only make out portions of the roof and backside of the cabin. At three hundred yards, he checked again and this time got the whole nasty scene in the crosshairs. Two dead deputies, single headshots at close range. One white male bent over the hood of a cruiser. Two more deputies holding him down while Sheriff Clemons raped him.

Jesus, he thought and lowered the rifle and swallowed a mouthful of disgust.

"What is it?"

Manny weighed how to tell her, even if he should tell her. Then he reasoned he had to. She'd trusted him, come with him this far, put her life in his hands. This wasn't the time to be hiding things because they were horrendous.

"The guy you were with, Russell, what's he look like?"

"White, skinny."

"Short hair?"

"Yeah."

Manny nodded. "The Sheriff got him."

"Good." Seph smiled but her sudden surge of happiness dimmed and the corner of her lips turned back down when she saw the look on Manny's face. "What? Is that who was screaming?"

"Yeah. He's the one crying right now."

"What are they doing to him?" Before he could answer her right hand shot up and covered her mouth. Her eyes bulged. "The grunting. He's being raped?"

Manny nodded.

"Oh my God."

"That's not all."

Her breath seemed to catch in her throat a second. "What do you mean?"

Manny rubbed his forehead. "There are two other deputies holding him down. But I don't think they have much choice."

"You always have a choice."

"That may be but I think the Sheriff has gone off the reservation."

"You think?"

Manny didn't appreciate the sarcasm. "There are two more deputies down there. Not the two holding Russell down. No, these two have gunshot wounds to the head."

"The Sheriff—"

"Yep."

"So what do we do?"

Manny patted the stock of the rifle. "I'll show you what we—"

His words were severed by shrieking howls. Manny lifted the scope to his eye. The Sheriff stood with his back arched and arms stretched toward heaven, howling at the moon. The other two deputies had backed away, no longer holding poor Russell.

Take your shot, Sniper, Manny thought. He lined the Sheriff's face in the crosshairs. His finger slid onto the trigger. He took a deep breath and held it and started to squeeze—

The Sheriff stepped back and waved a deputy forward, obstructing the shot.

"Shit."

"What?"

"Nothing. Just lost sight of things for a moment."

The Sheriff had fixed his clothes and watched as the deputies hiked Russell's pants back up and pull him off the hood and turn him around. Manny could hear their voices but couldn't make out the words. Then the Sheriff laughed and whipped the barrel across Russell's face. The deputies caught him and held him up. The Sheriff stepped forward and hit him in the gut. This time the deputies let him drop to the ground.

Manny tried to line up another shot but there was too much unpredictable movement. The Sheriff launched a boot into the side of Russell's face. Then stomped on his spine. Then bent over and laughed in the man's face before slapping him. Then he ordered the deputies to join the assault.

"Sounds like their killing him," Seph said.

"That about sums it up."

"Can you do something?"

"I can't get a clean shot. I may need to get closer."

"Don't leave me."

"I won't."

Russell was trying to roll away. The deputies kicked him as he did. The Sheriff followed, rubbing his crotch and howling here and there. They passed the cruiser and started down the driveway. Russell crawled now, arm over arm. The deputies were half-assing it now, kicking at his heels and elbows. No stomps. More like foot swipes. Ever few steps the Sheriff would run forward and mash down on his fingers or slap him in the back of the head. One time he spat on him.

Then they were out of view, down the driveway toward the Loop.

"Is he dead?"

"Not yet." Manny lowered the rifle and turned to her. "They're kicking him down the driveway."

She shook her head. "Russell's a son of a bitch but no one deserves this."

"I can go stop them. If you stay here—"

"Don't leave me alone."

"Do you want to get closer, see if we can do something?"

She nodded. "We should at least try, right?"

"Yeah." He shifted into a crouch. "We'll still move slow. No talking. Stay behind me and follow my lead. I'll use basic hand signals. Okay?"

"Okay."

"Let's go then."

BIGFOOT/BUNNY

It snorted everything he could find. What was left in the pipe. What was strewn on the ground. It licked the inside of the pipe clean. Not enough, though. Not enough.
    It tore through the tent. Found two more rocks. Gone. Still not enough. Needed more.
    It stomped around the site, sniffing, trying to catch a whiff of anything. Something. Something on the wind. But minute. Not here. No, all it smelled here was man scent. Woman scent. Spent seed.
    The woman on the ground, the one asleep, stirred. Her legs parted as she scratched between then. It watched. Watched her fingers rake the skin around her sex. Smelled her fluid.
    It reached down and touched its sex. Found it hardening. It moved to her.

Bunny's lips itched. She reached down and scratched. Probably got bit by something. Shouldn't have passed out in the dirt.
    But it'd been worth it. After watching the shower scene, she needed an escape. Needed to feel alive and she only felt alive in her dreams. On crank, they were so vivid. So real. Not like the real world. Not like her sad life.
    "Guy, you wouldn't believe the dream I had this time," she said, fluttering and wiping her eyes. "There was you and kitten and a monster. It—"
    She opened her eyes all the way. Something hovered over her. Something humongous. Inches from her face. Something ape-like.
    It took her another moment to realize it wasn't hovering. It was propped on its right elbow. The other hand was fumbling around somewhere out of sight. She felt it brush against her thighs. Between her thighs. Then something touched—

She started to scream but its left hand came up and clamped down on her mouth. It covered her nose and her left eye. She could still see with her right. See the frenzy in its eyes and it pushed.

Oh God, she thought.

It hurt. It hurt so badly. Even though she was wet it hurt. Enormous. Ripping her from the inside out.

Then it thrust deep and she almost lost consciousness. She could feel it in her stomach. Her ribs.

It grunted and thrusted. Faster. Harder. And finally, Bunny did lose consciousness. As she did she thought, *Nothing but filler.*

RUSSELL/GABE

"Now do us a favor," Gabe said. He leaned down close to Russell's face to make sure he heard him. "Don't go running off on us."

Russell groaned. Gabe laughed and rose. Then he kicked dirt and gravel in his face. It stuck to the blood and spit

"Let's go up and get ready for Bigfoot." Gabe turned and started back up the driveway.

"What about him?" Betts said.

Gabe turned and shrugged. "Kill him if you want."

"Are we just going to leave him?"

"We had our fun but we got more important fish to fry. The Foot will be here any minute. I can feel it."

"What if he runs off?"

"Does he look like he's running anywhere?"

"No, he doesn't," Pronger said. "Doesn't look like he'll be going anywhere for a long time."

"He'll probably bleed out right there." Gabe rubbed his crotch. "From his asshole or his face. Ha!" He pointed his gun at them. "Let's go, fuckers."

Betts held up his hands. "Ah, come on, Sheriff. You don't have to point that at us."

"Then start walking. You think I'm going to let you follow so you can put a round of your own in my back?"

"We wouldn't do that," Pronger said.

Gabe grinned. "Then you are fucking stupid. Let's go. If Russell's still alive when we're done with Bigfoot, maybe I'll give him one more dance before finishing him off. You hear that Russell?"

Russell groaned.

"See, he understands. Now how about you two prove you do, too, and get your asses moving."

***

Russell coughed and rolled onto his stomach. He couldn't see out of his left eye. Couldn't feel it move either. He didn't know if it was permanent or swelling had just closed it up. Pain raced up his sides like fire. Busted ribs for sure. Probably all of them. It hurt like hell to breathe. To move.

He pushed up to his knees and retched and vomited blood. When he did, agony smashed its way all the way down his spine to his ass. But he stayed on his knees. He refused to fall back on his face, no matter how much it hurt.

Because across from him was Mickey's Ford.

You can do this, he thought, blinking blood out of his right eye. He wiped it with the back of his hand and started to crawl toward the truck. Each time his knee hit gravel, it felt like a spike was driven into his thighs.

Keep moving, he thought. He couldn't tell how far the truck was. Too blurry. But it was getting closer.

Rocks dug into his palms. Blood filled his eye again. He wiped it away and gnashed his teeth and pressed on.

"Keep—" Moving his jaw was like getting hit with a sledge hammer. He shut up and thought, *Moving. Keep moving.*

He reached the front bumper. When he touched the cold metal, he almost cried.

Keep. Moving.

He grabbed the bumper with both hands and pulled up. Up. Up. Until he was standing, leaning on the hood.

Oh, God, he thought. *It hurts. Everything hurts so much.*

Then he realized where he was. The hood.

He spat and used the truck to brace himself up and moved around the side. Holding the fender. Holding the door. Holding the bed.

At the back bumper, he lowered into a squat and reached under. And found nothing.

No, he thought. *It's here. Mickey always kept it here.*

He clawed, fingers scratching metal and rust. It had to be here.

There!

He clenched a box and pulled it away and lifted it close to his good eye. The hideaway key.
Please let it still be in here, he thought. *Please.*
Russell slowly slid the box open, praying the whole way. A small glint of light reflected off a surface within. He reached in and lifted the key and tossed the box. Somehow he managed a smile. It didn't hurt too much. Then he grasped the bed and started making his way for the driver's door.

Gabe paced in a circle around the cruiser behind the cabin. "Where the fuck is it?"
Neither Betts or Pronger offered a response.
"You two opened the baggies, right?"
They nodded.
"Well, fuck!" Gabe stomped the dirt three times in rapid succession. "What the fuck kind of meth-Foot doesn't come running when the meth bell is ringing?"
"Maybe it died," Pronger said.
"From what?"
"We did shoot it. Maybe it bled out."
"No way." Gabe completed another lap. "No way. Not a beast like that. No way it's going out like a bitch." He pointed the gun at Lyle and Stanger. "Like these two."
"Speaking of them." Pronger swallowed hard and looked away from them. "Should we call the Coroner or something?"
"And tell him what? I killed them?"
"I didn't say that."
"How would you explain it then?"
"I don't know. I figured you have a plan."
"That's right. We're going to bury them."
"Bury them."
"Yep. Somewhere no one will find them. All the bodies got to go."
"The dealers, too."
"And Russell and that fuck Manny Lopez who called it in."
"Christ, Sheriff," Betts said. "You're going to kill Manny."
"Everyone who knows about this either kisses the ring—" He waved the gun at them. "Or dies. I don't think Manny's

125

a kissing ring kind of guy. So he shares a plot with these shitbirds for the rest of eternity."

"What about Debbie?" Pronger said. "She took the call. You wouldn't hurt her."

"That's right." Gabe reached down and rubbed his flaccid cock. Maybe he'd finally drained it dry. "Because she's going to kiss the ring and whatever else I tell her to."

Pronger shut up after that. Betts followed suit. Gabe considered adding them to the pile. One shot through each of their foreheads. Finish what he should have done long ago. But then he'd have to dig the graves. Nah. He'd make them do it. Then blow their fucking brains out and let them fall into the holes. Gabe didn't mind filling graves.

He scratched his neck and licked his lips. Could use some water. Water and another hit. Can't though. Bigfoot could be here any moment.

"Don't worry yourselves about any of them right now." Gabe scurried over to the entrance to the cellar and looked down. Maybe there was some more product down there. Some these dipshits missed. "Keep an eye out for Bigfoot. Yell if you hear it coming."

"Where are you going?" Pronger said.

"Down here real quick. Don't go running off or I'll find you and fucking kill you. And pin all this shit on your dead asses. Understand?"

"Sure thing, Sheriff," Betts said. "We're not going anywhere."

"Damn straight you're not." Gabe took the steps fast. "Because you don't want the Russell treatment. Ha!"

MANNY

The Sheriff moved in nervous circles. The deputies stood there with hands on hips and heads bowed. Defeated. Unwilling to even attempt a move on their insane leader. No Russell either. Probably finished him off somewhere on the driveway.

Enough of this shit, Manny thought and lined up the Sheriff's noggin from fifty feet away and to the right of the cabin, away from one mean drop down the backside hill. There was a body down there with its head smashed in against a tree. Probably one of the meth cookers.

Manny could hear the Sheriff talking about Bigfoot and not going out like a bitch. The rest he blocked out. Blocked out the nervous voices of the deputies. Blocked out Seph's shallow breathing behind him. It was just him and the target and a bullet. He zeroed in on the Sheriff and decided to put the round through his right eye. There ground was slightly lower than the back of the cabin but he didn't have to adjust much due to the short range of the shot. Just aim above the right eye and let speed and gravity do the rest.

"Send it." Chris's voice. Like he was right next to him. Manny smiled and held his breath and started to squeeze—

The Sheriff tracked away. Fast. Not running but damn close.

Manny adjusted and let the Sheriff lead him. He stopped at the back of the cabin and peered down. A cellar.

Back of the head is as good as the front, Manny thought.

"Elevation's still good," Chris said. "Send it."

On its way, he thought and squeezed—

The Sheriff's head snapped back around to his deputies.

Will you stop fucking moving for one second?

He lined up the right eye again and held his breath and squee—

The Sheriff bolted down the stairs into the cellar.

"Son of a bitch," Manny said, barely a whisper through clenched teeth.

"What happened?" Seph said.

"Took too long, Sniper," Chris said. "Can't hesitate. You know that."

"Yeah, yeah." Manny kept the scope trained on the cellar. *Next time his head pops up he's mine.*

"Yeah what?"

"Nothing. Just missed an opportunity. I won't again."

"You better not," Chris said.

BIGFOOT

It looked at what was left of the girl. Her sex bled. Her body twitched. It had gotten what it wanted but not what it needed. Still hungry. Needed to feed. Now. Its arms and chest burned around the wounds. Blood flowed here and there.

The woman had distracted it. Needed to move on. Find more food.

A strong gust of wind carried with it the scent of food. Heavy on the air. More than he'd smelled since fleeing.

It didn't wait. No time. Needed to feed. It sprinted, chasing the scent.

GABE/RUSSELL/MANNY

Gabe didn't find any more meth in the cellar. Instead, he found a bunch of Bigfoot shit. Piles of it from wall to wall. Flies everywhere. Holy Christ it stank.

In a good way. He chuckled and holstered his gun and clapped his hands together. In an oh so *gooood* way.

Gabe grabbed the top button of his shirt and undid it. Then the next and the next. All the way down. He stripped it off and threw it to the side.

"You ain't going to come to me?" He dropped his gun belt and pulled off his boots. "Fuck it. I'll find you."

His pants and jockeys followed the rest. He stood before a pile of runny shit and nodded. "Oh, yeah. I'm going to find you for sure. And you know what? You ain't even going to see me coming. Because I'm going to smell just like your hairy ass."

Gabe knelt and grabbed two handfuls of shit and rubbed it on his chest. "Woo! Just like Arnie in fucking *Predator*…"

…Russell sat behind the wheel, exhausted. He'd spent what little energy he had climbing into the truck. Now that he was in, he had a tough time fighting the clawing grasp of dreamland.

I got one shot, he thought. *It's them or me.*

He licked dried cracked lips and moved the key toward the ignition. It shook the whole way. When he reached it, he had to grab hold of his wrist with his free hand to ease it into the slot.

One shot.

Russell twisted the ignition and listened as the eight pistons turned and the first batch of injected fuel fired and the engine roared to life. He smiled. The greatest sound he'd ever heard.

He shifted into drive and eased on the gas and accelerated

and turned up the drive. He debated for a second how to make his approach.

"Fuck it."

Russell hit the high beams and floored it. The back tires spun, shooting gravel and dirt into the darkness. Then they bit and he flew…

…Manny heard an engine start. Toward the Loop.

"Was that a car?" Seph said.

"Yeah."

He shifted the scope to the deputies. They'd heard it to, both looking down the driveway.

"Maybe it was a neighbor," one of them said.

The other replied but Manny couldn't make it out. Too low.

Bright light illuminated the driveway from below. The engine screamed. The shadows of trees seemed to dance as the light grew closer and shifted with the contours of the drive.

"Someone's coming," Seph said.

"Yep, and fast."

The deputies still stood there, guns held out in front of them…

…Gabe finished smearing shit on his feet when he heard the engine. Muffled by the depth and walls of the cellar, it still sounded loud. Ferocious. Angry.

"Come get some, bitch."

Gabe slapped on his gun belt and grabbed the .38 and sprinted for the stairs…

…Manny shifted back to the cellar. A moment later a naked man, except for a gun belt and covered in mud, sprinted up into his crosshairs. It only took a split second for Manny to identify him as the Sheriff.

"Send it," Chris said.

Manny squeezed the trigger.

And closed his eyes.

The rifle kicked as the bullet exploded out of the barrel…

...A mule kicked Gabe's right shoulder. Then he heard the report and knew the truth. As he fell, he dropped his gun and pressed his hand against the wound. Blood met his palm.

He hit the ground and screamed as the pain registered...

...Manny opened his eyes and glassed the scene. The Sheriff was on the ground.

Fucking chickened out, Manny said. But you still managed to hit him.

A pang of intense guilt burned his gut until he noticed the Sheriff pawing at his shoulder and screaming. Both deputies had dropped into squats and pointed their guns toward the tree line. Eyes wide, panicked.

And the headlights and roaring engine completely forgotten.

"Holy shit," Seph said.

A Ford F-150 screamed around the back of the cabin and turned hard and painted the deputies with its high beams...

...Russell almost lost control of the truck. The back fishtailed but he managed to right it. The high beams lit up Betts and Pronger, crouched and turned toward the trees.

Wonder if they heard Bigfoot, he thought and laughed.

Their heads snapped in unison toward the truck. Their eyes caught the light like two deer on a country highway. Russell laughed some more...

...Manny watched as both deputies' heads snapped left in time to see the grill before the truck hit them and sucked them under. The driver slammed on the brakes before plowing into the berm. One body was caught up under the back tire and bumper. The other had cleared the truck, a pile of mangled bone and flesh bleeding out.

"Oh my God," Seph said. "He killed them. He killed them."

"Yes he did whoever he is." Manny lowered the scope. "Keep your voice down. We can't give our position away until we know—"

"It was Russell."

"What?"

"I saw him through the driver's window as he…ran over them."

Manny glanced over his shoulder at the idling truck. A white male with short hair behind the wheel, slumped to the side, his head leaning against the window. Yeah, it did look like Russell.

The Sheriff belted another scream. Manny glassed him. He rolled side-to-side on his back, left hand clenching his right shoulder. Based on the audible pain, Manny figured the bullet destroyed the Sheriff's collar bone and part of his shoulder blade.

"What do we do now?" Seph said.

Manny lowered the rifle and looked around the woods. "I don't think we have to worry about Bigfoot."

"You don't?"

"No. After all this, he probably went as far away in the opposite direction as he could."

"It's hooked on meth though."

"I think it'll be okay."

Seph looked over Manny's shoulder at the truck. "You think he's dead?"

"Maybe. We should go check."

The Sheriff screamed again. About half as loud as the others. Succumbing to shock and blood loss.

"And the Sheriff?"

Manny frowned. "We'll check on him, too."

BIGFOOT

It found the food. Twisting up through the wood. One after another, scattered on the ground. In the bushes. Leading toward home. It fed and walked and fed and walked. It paid no attention to the sounds of pain and ruin. It didn't care. It only wanted to eat.

MANNY

The Sheriffs screams faded to whimpers. Manny was amazed the son of a bitch hadn't lost consciousness by now based on the shock and amount of blood lost. Then again, crazy fuckers tended to be surprisingly resilient.

Maybe I'll get lucky and the bastard will bleed to death, he thought.

Manny and Seph stepped out of the trees into the backyard of the cabin. She stayed close to him, hand cupped in the crook of his left elbow. They moved past the cruiser and the deputies who had been shot in the head. Past the mangled body. Manny was surprised Seph didn't choke or vomit. He didn't know the scope of death she'd been exposed to in her life but this scene would make hardened combat vets check their guts. She gave no indication it bothered her in the least. Just determined to reach Russell.

They reached the back of the truck and the last body, folded in half under the tire and bumper. Seph let go of his arm then and hurried to the driver's door. She tapped on the glass and said Russell's name several times.

Manny checked the Sheriff again to make sure he wasn't all of the sudden up and moving like the crazy fucker he was. Satisfied he wasn't going anywhere probably ever again, he slung the rifle over his shoulder and moved over to Seph's side.

"You open the door and I'll catch him," he said. "Then we'll pull him out together."

"Okay."

Seph gripped the handle and lifted and pulled. Manny stepped forward and caught the slouching body in his arms. He hooked both hands under the armpits and held fast until Seph was able to get her arms around Russell's calves.

"One, two, three, lift," Manny said.

He pulled and she lifted and they managed to maneuver Russell out of the truck without any trouble. They carried him a few feet away and eased him to the ground. Once there, Manny pressed two fingers against Russell's carotid artery.

"Is he alive?"

Manny nodded. He looked Russell's body over. Face mashed up. Blood clotting from wounds to his eyes, nose, and mouth. Probably a half-dozen busted ribs. He refused to imagine the damage to Russell's rectum. "Whether that's good or bad I don't know."

"We need to get him to a hospital."

"Yeah, we do. First, though, we need to figure out what to do about him." Manny jerked a thumb at the Sheriff. "My original plan didn't work out too well."

Seph looked over at the Sheriff. "How'd you miss?"

"I couldn't do it." Manny rubbed his face. "I can't do it anymore."

"Bad stuff happened over there, huh?"

"Over there?" Manny smirked. "You could say that."

"Maybe we call the cops."

"More cops?"

"Highway Patrol or something. County Sheriff."

Manny looked back at the Sheriff. "Or we leave him here. Let him die."

"Could you live with that?"

"Hell, I don't know. I'm not sure what I can live with after this."

"So you'd let someone suffer and die and not do anything about it?"

"You really threw that back in my face quick, didn't you?"

Seph sighed. "Not trying to. We do need to do something. But we also need to make sure all this points back to him."

"He can't pin it on us."

"No but he needs to go to jail for the rest of his life and we need more witnesses than us."

"Russell, if he lives." Manny looked around the cabin. "There are only a few people on the Loop this time of year. Since we haven't seen or heard anyone else, I think we can assume there's either no one else here or they're hiding. Killing him would have been the easiest way."

"Will you two fucking pussies shut the fuck up already?" The Sheriff waved a bloody hand at them and flicked them off. "Let me die in piece."

Manny motioned with his head. "Let's go say hi."

They left Russell and walked over to the Sheriff. Manny shifted the rifle from his shoulder to his hands and leveled it on the lawman. As they closed, they noticed a stench rising from him. Harsher and harsher until it was almost burning their eyes. He wasn't covered in mud but feces.

Manny kicked the revolver further away and stood at the Sheriff's side and aimed the barrel at his shit-smeared forehead.

The Sheriff laughed. "I already heard you weren't going to kill me. Fucking pussy Marine. Lost your nutsack over in Iraq, huh? Can't even hurt a fly anymore."

Manny ignored the taunts and said, "You're the one bleeding out from my round."

"Lousy fucking shot, too." More laughter followed by a moan and grasping the shoulder. "Shooting me in the dick would have hurt less."

"I still can if you want me to."

"Fuck off."

"I think I'm going to puke," Seph said around the hand covering her nose and mouth. "Why are you covered in shit?"

"Thought he was going to mask his scent," Manny said. "You really think that was going to work?"

"You're a fucking smart Mexican, aren't you?"

"Costa Rican on my father's side, turd boy."

"I can't take anymore of this stench," Seph said. "I'm going to go back over to Russell."

The Sheriff fluttered his eyes, shifting from Manny to Seph. "Hey, I know you."

"I don't see how."

The Sheriff laughed and pointed with his good hand. "You're Wheezy's girl."

Manny watched as Seph's face slacked. Her hand dropped

to her side and her lower lip trembled just a bit.

"What do you know about Wheezy?"

"Wouldn't you like to know."

Seph picked up the Sheriff's revolver, ignoring the shit-smeared grip, and cocked it and pointed it at his face. "Tell me."

"Or what, you'll kill me. Thought you wanted me to pay for what I've done."

Manny recognized the blind anger starting to burn in Seph's eyes. If he didn't do something quick, she'd lose control and shoot him for sure. He leaned in and jammed the barrel into the shoulder wound hard. The Sheriff belted a wail and grabbed the barrel and tried to yank it away. Manny pushed harder.

"Tell her what she wants to know." He lifted the barrel away. "Or I'll do it again."

"Okay, okay," he said around heavy breaths. "I know he was a fucking pot dealer in my town. *Was* being the appropriate word." He laughed. "Know his asshole was tighter than Russell's there. I made a bum rape him first. But once the other deputies were gone, I took my turn. Shot a big old load up there. Then I beat the living shit out of him and dumped him in the woods off of Route 3."

"Is he dead?"

"Don't know. Haven't seen or heard anything about him. Guessing you haven't either. Maybe you should take a drive out there. Might find him waiting for you."

"You son of a bit—"

Manny settled his hand on her arm before she pulled the trigger and said, "Wait."

The Sheriff laughed some more. "At least she has more balls than you, Manny."

"Let me," Seph said, not looking at him.

"If you do, you'll have to carry it around the rest of your life. I won't stop you but you have to be sure you can carry that load."

"I can. For Wheezy."

Manny studied her for a moment. The lower lip no longer trembled. Her face had hardened. Eyes narrow. Jaw set. She could. At least she believed she could. Sometimes nothing else was needed.

"Okay." Manny released her arm and stepped back and watched.

"How'd you end up here anyway?" the Sheriff said.

"I was in the valley, saying goodbye to Wheezy when Russell came running through with Bigfoot behind him."

"Don't that just take the cake. Me the one who ended Wheezy's business and possibly his life here and you're here and poor old Russell over there being the string that kind of brought us together."

"And me holding your gun. The gun that's going to kill you."

The Sheriff laughed again. Full of mock and contempt. "Shit, you can't do it. I can see it in your eyes. Sure you're pissed and no doubt you wouldn't shed a tear if Manny the pussy there pulled the trigger. But watching and doing are two vastly different things. You're not the doing type. You're too…normal."

"You don't know a fucking thing about me."

"Sure I do. I know you didn't file a missing person's report. Didn't want to get Wheezy into trouble just in case he was okay somewhere. Figured after a while he left town. Maybe for another woman. Maybe because you did something to piss him off recently. Either way you decided to keep quiet and hope he came back. When he didn't, you came out here to say goodbye. You loved him sure. But you didn't have any problem letting go either. That's what normal people do. They resign themselves to the easier of two choices. Killing ain't easy."

Seph's jaw flexed. Her grip on the gun tightened. She refused to blink.

But then her hand started to shake. Slight at first but more noticeable with every passing second. When the barrel moved side-to-side and up-and-down, the Sheriff beamed.

"Told you."

Seph eyes lifted to Manny's. "I can't."

"I can."

Both turned to find Russell on his knees crawling toward them.

139

BIGFOOT

It reached the end of the trail. Couldn't find anymore. Couldn't find any more food. Still hungry. Need food. Need it to stop the pain.
    Need food now!
    NEED TO FEED!

GABE/RUSSELL/MANNY

"Where'd you hide the key to that truck?" the Sheriff said.
"Hideaway under the back bumper."
"Son of a bitch. Never thought to search the truck."
"Yeah, you should have you stupid bastard." Russell stopped crawling when he reached the dude with the rifle and Seph. "Can you help me up?"
They reached under his arms and hoisted. Russell managed to push with his legs. Everything still hurt but not nearly as bad as before. Had to be…what did athletes call it…endorphins or something. Maybe adrenaline. Definitely a high of some kind.
"Are you okay?" Seph said.
Russell cocked his head toward her. The anger toward him was gone. She looked genuinely concerned. "No but I think I'll live."
"I'm sorry."
"You didn't do anything to me. He did."
"But—"
"Leaving me was the smart move." Russell pointed at the rifleman. "You ended up with a guy with a gun. If you would have stuck with me, who knows what this piece of shit would have done to you."
The Sheriff tried to sit up but only made it a few inched before falling back down and groaning. "You liked it punk."
Russell spat on him, a mix of blood and saliva.
"You want to do this?" Seph offered him the revolver.
Russell lingered on it a moment, wondering if he'd be able to hold it let alone aim and shoot it. "Yeah."
He took it and shuffled forward and stopped next to the injured shoulder of the Sheriff. He gazed down at the shit-covered man. Relived everything he'd done to him in a three second flash. Then he aimed the already cocked revolver at

his head.

"What you ain't going to pay the favor back?" the Sheriff said. "Not going to stick the barrel up my ass or make me suck you off as you press it against by head or—"

A roar cut him off. From behind them. From the tree line. Russell didn't have to turn to know what it was. It was the same damn friend roar he'd heard earlier as it chased him. He closed his eyes, almost surrendering. Accepting that he'd lost even though he'd made it this far.

He heard feet stomping hard against the earth. Pounding. He heard light feet twisting, pivoting on the gravel. He heard the rifleman yelling at Seph to get back. He heard the rifle discharge...

...Manny had it. Had it dead to rites as it burst from the tree line.

"Send it!" Chris yelled in his head.

Manny squeezed the trigger. Squeezed it without closing his eyes.

But the round missed, hitting the beast the right deltoid. It was closing too fast and he hadn't accounted for the rapidly narrowing distance between them. The bullet slowed it down, though, knocking it back a few feet. Slowed it enough to line-up another shot...

...Gabe didn't wait any longer. Bigfoot was coming and this was his last chance. Then Russell gave him the easy opening he needed. The stupid motherfucker closed his eyes while everyone else turned to see the Foot charging at them.

Ha-ha, motherfucker!

He grabbed the pepper spray from his belt and gritted through the pain and sat up...

...Russell heard, "Suck on this, motherfucker!"

Russell opened his eyes in time to see the Sheriff sitting up with pepper spray can extended toward his face, no more than six inches away. Then the blast hit him and the world turned red...

…Manny heard the Sheriff yell behind him. Then the pepper spray discharge. He'd seen it on the lawman's belt and hadn't thought to disarm him with all the commotion over Seph. Another stupid mistake.
"Blink your eyes," Manny said and lined up another shot. "Both of you."
Bigfoot clutched its deltoid and roared in pain more than in anger. It didn't stay immobile for long, locking on Manny and charging. Manny blinked tears as the pepper spray drifted around his head. He'd been trained to deal with it. The key was not to panic. Blink. Let the tears lubricate the eyes. But it still burned like hell. The eyelids. The cheeks.
He swallowed a cough and fired but his vision had blurred significantly due to the spray. He heard the bullet hit flesh and another wail of pain but couldn't see the impact.
"I can't see!" Seph screamed.
Manny could but barely. He found Bigfoot again, on one knee, clutching its gut. He lined up for a final shot when he heard, "Can you see me now, motherfucker…"

…Russell pawed at his face, trying to scrape the pepper spray from his eyes. It seemed to blaze a trail all the way down his optic nerves. Salt filled his mouth from the tears streaming down his cheeks. He could see nothing but blurs and smears. Then the spray made it into his throat and ignited his lungs. He doubled over and coughed and coughed, his chest tightening to the point of suffocating.
Another roar. This time fury mixed with pain. New pain. Followed by another rifle shot.
Something hit him. Hard. The blurs and smears rotated around him. His back hit the ground. What little air he had forced into his lungs raced out of him. The gun fell from his hand.
The Sheriff jumped on him, the smell of shit filling his nose. Thumbs press against his eyes. Hard and deep. The burn was replaced with the pain of compression. Of his eyes being pushed into the back of his skull.
"Can you see me now, motherfucker!"

Russell screamed and flailed. When his eyeballs popped, he shrieked so loud it could cut granite. Then he felt something in his mouth. Being pushed down, down. Past his tongue. Into his throat. His nose being pinched shut.

No air. Gurgling. But soon it faded. It all faded. The pain. The burning. It all went away.

And so did everything else...

...Manny could only see a blurred image of the Sheriff, kneeling on Russell's chest, destroying his eyes with his thumbs. But it was enough to hit and save Russell's life.

Seph screamed behind him.

Manny didn't hesitate, spinning to find her, expecting to see Bigfoot readying to tear her arms out. But instead, he found her lying on her side. She'd run into Russell's truck.

"Shit."

Bigfoot was still on its knee, clutching its gut.

Manny spun back to Russell and found the Sheriff shoving the can of pepper spray down his throat. He lined up the shot and fired.

Click.

Shit!

Misfire. Manny went to chamber another round.

The Sheriff was rising, revolver in hand. No time to finish chambering and get a shot. Manny ran and dove behind the truck before he could spin around...

...Gabe pushed the can of pepper spray as far down Russell's throat as he could. He pinched his nose and leaned down into his ear and whispered sweet nothings until Russell quit jerking and flailing. It didn't take long. Once he was done, he rose and spun around, revolver in his hand, looking for Manny.

But Manny wasn't there. Gone. "Ran off, huh. Fucking coward!"

Seph had run into the car and lay on her side, holding her leg with one hand and rubbing her eyes with the other. Bigfoot knelt, shoulders rising and falling on heavy breaths.

And here I stand, triumphant, Gabe thought. His shoulder

had numbed and that arm hung loose. It had worked when he needed it but now it was no use. He held the revolver with his good hand, extended out in front of him, trained on Bigfoot's huge melon.

He started to squeeze the trigger but his hand shook and he could keep it straight enough to get a clean shot. The pepper spray fucked with him, too, causing everything to blur. "Shit."

Fuck it, he thought. *Only one way to be sure.*

He walked over, slowly, ready to put two through Bigfoot's eyes…

…Manny knelt behind Russell's truck. He'd chambered another round and peered over the top of the bed at the Sheriff. The crazy fucker was walking up to the Bigfoot. He was actually going to shoot it up close.

More power to him, Manny thought and braced his elbows on the bed of the truck and lined up the shit-smeared head of the Sheriff in the crosshairs. Still blurry but a fat target impossible to miss…

…Gabe stood before the Foot. Not scared. Hell, he felt righteous. Mighty. Man versus Nature be damned. Man conquers mother fucking Nature.

"Look at me," Gabe said and looked down the barrel at Bigfoot's hanging head.

It didn't listen. Didn't move. Just sat there, wheezing, holding its guts in. Gabe rapped the barrel across its head.

"Look at me, you big fucking monkey."

Bigfoot's head started to lift, little by little. Its forehead. His thick brow. Then its eyes. No longer furious. No longer fiend-like. Just two dots full of tears.

"Ah, is the little fucking monkey in pain?" Gabe grabbed his dick. It was semi-hard. "Sad you got beat by a real man?"

Bigfoot watched him. No change in facial features. No recognition of what was about to happen to him. Just a sad heap of a fucking ape.

"Time to say bye bye." Gabe smiled. "Here comes Gabe's huge payday."

Bigfoot's left hand shot up from his side and clenched Gabe's balls and dick and squeezed before he could fire. The sudden burst of horrendous pain caused his back to arch and his arms to shoot out to his sides as if crucified. Then he felt the tearing...

...Manny watched, smile on his face, as Bigfoot ripped the Sheriff's balls and dick off and tossed them to the side. Watched as the Sheriff fell to the ground, yowling like a cat in heat, cupping his bloody groin, kicking walking in a circle in the gravel, forming concentric circles of blood as he curled tighter and tighter into a fetal position.

Bigfoot rose, one hand still holding its stomach. It looked down at the Sheriff. Looked like he was studying him. Then its head turned and found Manny. It stared right up the scope into Manny's eyes and for the second time that night, he felt as if an animal was staring into his soul.

This time though, Manny sent it.

The bullet tore through Bigfoot's forehead and blew out the back of its head in a spray of pink mist. It stood there a moment, swaying. Then it crumpled, falling on the Sheriff, pinning down to bleed out.

That's the first thing you've done right all night, Manny thought. *And it let you.*

He'd take it.

He pushed away from the truck and lowered the rifle. He circled around and found Seph sitting, watching it all.

"Are you okay?" he said.

"Yeah. Eyes still hurt but not as bad."

"It doesn't last long and we didn't get a full blast like Russell. We were lucky."

"And Russell?"

"Not so lucky."

Seph nodded. She held out a hand and Manny grabbed it and helped her to her feet. She looked around a moment. At the carnage. The Sheriff still yowled. Not as loud now. He wouldn't last much longer with that amount of blood loss.

"Sounds like a goner," Seph said.

"You could say that."

"Not fast enough, though."

Manny started ask what she meant but she was already moving. She walked to the side of the one of the dead deputies and grabbed his revolver. Checked it to make sure it had rounds. Then she walked over to the Sheriff, pinned under Bigfoot's corpse, sobbing, aimed and fired.

"Now what?" she said, still looking at her work.

Manny looked around him for a moment before saying, "We burn it all."

MANNY

Seph and Manny moved the bodies into the cellar. First the deputies and then Mickey and his arms and the guy with the glasses. Then Russell. Manny didn't like dumping him in with the others but there was no other choice.

When it came time to haul up the guy who became one with a tree, Manny dug a rope out of the garage and climbed down the hill and tied it around the ankles and pulled him up. Manny wasn't sure he'd be able to get him all the way up the steep incline on his own but he did.

The Sheriff they did second to last. Manny dug his bullet out of the shoulder wound first. Then they tied the rope around his ankles and yanked him down the stairs into the cellar to keep from getting Bigfoot shit all over them.

When it came time to move Bigfoot, Manny decided to use the truck to tow him to the top of the cellar. They tried rolling it from there but the beast was too heavy. Manny figured top of the cellar was good enough.

Done with the bodies, Manny grabbed a shovel and bucket from the garage and scooped up all the brain matter and blood-soaked dirt he could and dumped it in with the deceased. They moved in grim silence. Manny knew what he was doing. Seph was good at following orders. Efficient.

Manny siphoned gas from the truck's tank into another bucket and went about dousing parts inside and around the cabin. Siphoned more and repeated the process for the cop cars and the truck. And finally Bigfoot's body.

"Okay, we're done," Manny said. "I need to light the fires and haul ass."

"Where are we going?"

"My place first. After that it's up to you."

"I don't know what to do after."

"Split town. Today. The farther away the better."

"I thought this would cover us."

"It will but it doesn't mean we should stick around to find out. I'm pretty much off the grid except for a few bills. Got any issues keeping you from hitting the road?"

She shook her head. "My car's still down there in the valley. Maybe pick-up a few things from my apartment."

"Is it in your name?"

"No, it's in Wheezy's. Lease is up next month and I was going to move out anyway."

"Then I recommend we head to my place. Once dawn breaks, we'll head on our merry ways."

"What about my car?"

"We'll grab it on the way."

"Okay. I don't know where I'll go but okay."

"I'll get the fires going. Head into the woods and I'll catch up."

Manny washed his hands and dried them and then stepped out on the balcony and peered across the valley. Dawn had come. Smoke still rose from the cabin but nowhere near as bad as before. A dying fire.

He turned on his police scanner. The county Sheriff was on the scene apparently. Fire was ninety percent out but he was requesting a coroner and county crime lab personnel.

Need to hit the road, Manny thought and walked back into the cabin.

"How is it out there?" Seph sipped coffee.

"Fires almost out."

"That's good."

"County Sheriff's on the scene and requesting crime lab people."

"That's bad."

Manny shrugged. "Not great but it's going to take time to make sense of what they have in that cellar. Our biggest problem will be deputies going door-to-door taking statements. Once the confusion wears off, they'll come knocking. Might even set-up a check point at the front of the Loop."

"So we need to get moving."

"Yep. We should probably hit the road here in about ten minutes."

"We as in together or separate?"

Manny scratched the counter with his fingernail. "Well, together I guess unless you got somewhere else to go."

"Are you asking me to go with you?"

Manny shrugged and wiped away flaked up pieces of ketchup. "I think we make a pretty good team."

"I'm not a sniper buddy."

"You mean spotter and I didn't mean it that way."

"How did you mean it?"

"I don't know. Maybe, if the circumstances were different, I'd ask you to dinner. Instead, I'm asking you if you want to go to Montana. Give me a break."

Seph smiled. "That's the oddest way I've ever been asked on a date."

"Got a better idea?" Manny smiled albeit a bit sheepish. "I'm willing to listen."

"No, I don't have a better idea." She moved to the counter. "And I don't have anywhere to go. So, yeah, I'll go to Montana with you. No promises after that, though."

Manny met her eyes. It was the first time he really looked at them in the light. Light blue. Almost sky blue. "Play it by ear?"

"Play it by ear."

Manny nodded. Smiled. Then he motioned at the bag of money on the counter. "At least we don't have to worry about how to divvy that up right now."

EPILOGUE

"It's not real."

"Fuck you, it so is."

Daniel studied his roommate, eyes glued to his computer screen, watching for the millionth time as "Bigfoot" supposedly rapes some chick in the middle of the woods. He didn't know how Kurt stomached it. Or why it fascinated him so much. Yet it did. Kurt, without a doubt, loved watching Bigfoot fuck this girl to death.

"How can it be real?" Daniel said. "Look at the angles. Camera's crooked and on its side. Worst possible angle to see. Grainy night vision and slightly out of focus. So you really can't see its face or the zipper that probably runs down the front of the suit. Plus the girl's a pro. A few news sites have already confirmed she's an amateur porn star. Put two and two together, man. It's a helluva a hoax but still a hoax."

"No way, man. You can't fake this."

On the screen, Bigfoot pounded away between the girl's legs. She was already unconscious or dead, head canted away from the camera. Again, convenient.

"You know how I know it's real?"

"How, Kurt?"

"Right here. Check it out."

Daniel frowned but looked over Kurt's shoulder at the screen. Bigfoot rose. The girl's crotch groin came into view. Blood that looked black in the night vision soaked her vagina and the inside of her thighs and her midsection.

"Fake blood," Daniel said.

"Not that." Bigfoot turned. As he did, its giant erect dick swung into view. Kurt pointed at it as if he were witnessing a miracle. "That! You can't fake a dick that big."

Daniel smirked and patted him on the shoulder. "Well,

you've got me there. Can't fake a big dick."

"Ah, screw you. You know it's real."

"Keep telling yourself that," Daniel said as he walked out of the dorm room.

ERIK WILLIAMS is a Defense Contractor, former Naval Officer, Iraq War Veteran, and former Kenpo Karate instructor. He is the author of *Bigfoot Crank Stomp*, *Progeny*, *Demon*, and numerous short stories. He has three daughters and is undergoing testosterone treatments to continue to feel like a man. Learn more about him at www.erikwilliams.blogspot.com or follow him on Twitter @TheErikWilliams

Milton Keynes UK
Ingram Content Group UK Ltd.
UKHW021317311023
431669UK00024B/1056